**TANDEM**

The Casbah Killers

"Nick Carter is a super-intelligence agent *par excellence*. He is close to superhuman. . . . Six-foot-plus of whipcord strength, and he has something in his head besides bone. Like all good spies, he has an almost phenomenal memory; a knowledge of many places, people, enemy weaponry and techniques, and odd little bits of information that he has tucked away for future reference.

"And he loves women. He doesn't just *love* sex, he *enjoys* it enormously; but he really loves women. He prefers to like the ones he goes to bed with . . . and he does not keep eager women waiting."
*New York Times*

# The Casbah Killers

Nick Carter

**TANDEM**
14 Gloucester Road, London SW7

Originally published in the United States by Universal
Publishing & Distributing Corporation, 1969

Published in Great Britain by Universal-Tandem Publishing
Co. Ltd, 1970
Reprinted 1971

*Dedicated to*
*The Men of the Secret Services*
*of the*
*United States of America*

Made and printed in Great Britain by
Hunt Barnard Printing Ltd., Aylesbury, Bucks.

# CHAPTER 1

The damned rubber raft wouldn't paddle. It was like sitting on a roller coaster in Coney Island in the middle of the night. Only the roller coaster was wet, it wasn't Coney Island but the coastline of Morocco and the pre-dawn, inky blackness of a moonless night, some five or so miles above the port of Casablanca.

I'd been told that not so very long ago, before the Delure jetty was built, steamers stopping at Casablanca always anchored far offshore. Passengers were lowered in wicker baskets to bobbing, over-crowded bumboats for the trip to shore. Capsizings were frequent, shattered nerves a certainty and I was getting an idea what they went through. Long underwater sandbars and heavy seas made most of the Moroccan coastline on the Atlantic a constant succession of towering swells and rolling breakers.

My little rubber raft rose up on the crest of every swell and then came down into the trough with a roar of wind and foam, only to be lifted up again instantly on the rise of the next one. I'd been lowered —raft, equipment and me—from one of the big Marine 'copters from the carrier Saratoga. I wore a tight, one-piece oilskin, not unlike a frogman's suit, over my clothes. In the raft was a small knapsack and a bundle, both wrapped in the waterproof covering.

The tide and the sea were conspiring to carry me in and paddling was mostly an empty gesture. I was grateful that the coastline was sandy and not rockbound. When I waved off the huge 'copter and watched it disappear into the blackness, its running lights turned off, it had seemed like such a simple ride into shore. And then I passed over the first of the underwater sandbars and the raft rose up and seemed to skitter out from under me. The rest had been a constant battle to stay upright. But now I could make out the dark outline of the coast, the slow rise of the sandy areas back from the shore.

Unlike the spread-out cities of the American coastline, the sprawling, overlapping areas sociologists have termed "megalopolis," the cities of Morocco and the other north and west African lands are enclaves unto themselves. Once past the city boundaries one was in primitive land, desert or shore, where only small villages and solitary settlements dotted the land. It was such a lone and solitary stretch of coastline we had picked to set me ashore. I say "we," but what I mean is the super-efficient planning operations staff of AXE headquarters.

I was keeping a sharp eye out for lights of any sort. Casablanca, and the adjacent area, of course, was a mecca of its own, a crossroads port where every kind of contraband found its way, where every type of smuggling flourished, where every imaginable illicit traffic found an avenue for itself. Consequently, the authorities kept two-way coastal patrols, the one onshore using jeeps and horses, the one offshore using World War II PT boats, reconditioned and refurbished. But it stayed dark and, I found out the hard way, I was too busy watching for the wrong things.

I was coming close inshore now and the raft was lifted again, swept in on a strong swell until a sandbar rose up to catch the bottom and I was pitched forward and halfway out. I managed to hang on, spit out a mouthful of salt water, and flipped over the side, pulling the raft onto the stretch of sand.

I found a ridge topped by a growth of eelgrass and sea scrub which made a convenient hedge. I sat down, pulled off the one-piece oilskin coverall, took the material from the bundle and the knapsack, piled it all into the raft and then used my lighter to set it afire. It burned quickly without flaring, a specially treated material that oxydized with amazing speed so that in minutes there was nothing left, not a burnt scrap nor a charred ash. Nothing. The stuff would self-destruct in minutes I'd been told by Special Effects, and I gave a slight nod to the efficiency as I watched the subdued flame.

It took only that, a few minutes and in that short space of time, Nick Carter, AXE Agent N3, had vanished and in his place stood Glen Travis, artist, painter, replete with paint box, brushes, palette, corduroy trousers and open-necked beige shirt. Inside the paint box was a full array of colors, tubes of the newer acrylic-based paints and each tube, in its own way, a masterpiece.

Of course, not many artists carried Wilhelmina, my 9mm Luger in a special shoulder holster, nor Hugo, the pencil-thin stiletto strapped in its sheath to my forearm. In a small knapsack I had a few changes of clothing and an American passport impeccably doctored to make it read that I'd just crossed through Algeria.

The sky was beginning to lighten ever so slightly and with paint box in hand, I walked up a sandy ridge to turn and look back at the darkness of the sea and the fading night stars. I guess Glen Travis, the artist, had taken over a little too much because all I heard, at the last moment, was the faint, whistling sound.

I whirled and got the rock smack against the temple. I glimpsed the end of a string and then all went into blazing yellows and purples. I remember thinking that this was impossible, that no one could have known of my coming.

The second blow did away with what little consciousness I had left. I went down into the sand and lay there. It was daylight when I woke, and my head hurt with a throbbing pain. I forced my eyes open, and even that slight effort hurt.

My mouth was gritty and tasted of sand, and I used my tongue to wipe some of it from my lips and gums. I spit it out and shook my head to clear it. Slowly, a room came into focus, if you could call it a room. I was alone and my wrists hurt, and I realized they were tied behind my back. A door, half off its hinges and open, was directly across from where I sat on the floor. Through it, I could glimpse the sea beyond. Obviously, I wasn't far from where I'd arrived. I let my eyes roam around the room.

A broken-down table, two equally broken-down chairs and some worn, sheepskin hassocks accounted for most of the furnishings. Another, smaller room led from the one where I was and I saw what seemed to be rolled-up bedding on the floor.

I tried to remember what had happened but all I could recollect was a glimpse of the rock and a dim realization that it was at the end of a length of string. It was a primitive but highly effective weapon, and I suddenly saw Hawk's face across the desk from me in his office at AXE Headquarters in Washington, D.C.

"It's a funny place, Morocco," he had said. "I was stationed there for a while, during the last war. I was in Casablanca when Roosevelt and Churchill met there and tried to get de Gaulle and Giraud to work together. It's a real crossroads of the world, Morocco, where the past lives in the present and the present never forgets the past.

There are some places, some ports, that through geography or local characteristics, seem to attract everything and everyone. They're real wastebaskets of the world's scroungy characters. Hong Kong is one, Marseille is another, New Orleans used to be one and Casablanca is certainly one. It's very tourist-conscious in some spots and very ninth-century in others."

"Obviously you expect trouble," I had said. "This cover you've dreamed up and Special Effects."

"We don't know what you might run into. All we know is that Karminian has been a top contact, always with good stuff, always reliable. Like the others of his kind, we had to pay for what he brought to us, but he was damned helpful."

I was recalling how Hawk's steel-blue eyes had clouded and the small furrow traced its way across the weathered, New England farmer's countenance. "Watch yourself," he had said. "It's a funny place full of unexpected things."

I winced and his face swam away and I was gazing out the empty doorway again. I yanked at the ropes holding my hands behind my back. They gave, slightly, and at once I knew that I could be free in seconds if I could get them against something halfway sharp. The rusted, broken hinge on the door would do it.

I was about to get on my feet when I saw the two figures appear in the doorway, the first one carrying in a goatskin water bag. He was dressed in the traditional *serwal*, the loose, baggy trousers that tapered to hug the calves and a cotton shirt.

His companion wore the loose and more common one piece coverall garment called the *djellaba*. Each wore a tattered *fez*. They were a scroungy, seedy pair and the first one had only one eye, the other eye being a shriveled and closed hole in his head.

"Ah, our pigeon has awakened," he said with relish as he put down the goatskin bag. The second one, taller and thinner, munched on a handful of grapes and spit the seeds out through clenched teeth. He was carrying my paint box, and he dropped it on the floor with the obvious distaste of a thief who'd found something utterly useless to him.

The one-eyed one came to stand in front of me, his face a leathery, wizened piece of parchment.

"You have little money," he said. "That we have discovered already." He spoke in poor French but good enough to understand. As my French was a lot better than my Arabic, I went along with him.

"Why do you want to rob a poor painter?" I asked. "An artist on his way to Casablanca to find work."

He smiled, a ragged, evil smile. His one good eye held more than enough craftiness for two.

"You are not a poor artist," he said. "Someone will pay a lot of money for you. You will tell us who and we shall sell you to them."

Ransom for a prisoner, one of the most ancient and time-honored devices in the Moslem lands. Chiefs ransomed their important prisoners. Kings ransomed opposing princes. Thieves held rich men for ransom. I hadn't figured anybody was expecting me, and now I was certain my assumptions were right. These two were nothing but crafty opportunists who had seen me arrive and were going to make the most of it.

I tossed out another denial to reconfirm my cover.

"I'm just an artist," I said. "An American painter."

"A poor artist does not arrive by the dark of the night in stealth on a raft from the sea and then erase his footsteps by fire," the one-eyed one answered craftily.

I met his cunning stare grimly. There was no doubt in my mind any longer. These two were nothing but the Moroccan version of a couple of muggers who happened to be at the right spot at the right time.

"It was unfortunate for you that you chose to come ashore right across from this little place where we happen to be staying," the one-eyed one said. He smiled, pleased with himself.

I had some bad news for him. Maybe it had been a bit of rotten luck for me, but it would turn out to be fatal for him and his cohort. I couldn't afford to leave anyone around to tell stories of the man they'd seen arriving by sea in a raft.

These two miserable creatures, in their own scurrilous desire for the fast buck, had just committed a form of suicide. They had sealed their own fate. Wilhelmina still nestled in the shoulder holster and Hugo was still securely strapped to my arm. Like most third-class thieves, they weren't even good at their own profession. The one with the grapes came over to stand in front of me.

I watched him draw back his foot, take careful aim and kick out, the blow catching me in the pit of the stomach. Waves of nauseous pain swept over me and I doubled forward. I stayed that way, letting the waves of pain slowly recede. The bastard. The stupid bastard. If I'd had any qualms about what I had to do they'd just disappeared. I felt his hands pulling me back upright.

"Who is expecting you, son of a sow?" he asked.

I reminded myself that both hands were still firmly behind my back. Taking on both of them from this position would be a little much.

"In the sand at the beach," I gasped out. "Where I landed. There is a tube pressed down there, a small tube. Get it. It will tell you what you want to know."

The one-eyed one spoke quickly to the other in Arabic. The taller one dashed out, the *djellaba* flying behind him, his thin legs churning.

I watched till he disappeared behind the sand ridge beyond the doorway. As soon as he was out of sight, I spoke to the other one, putting urgency and stealth in my voice.

"Let me go and I'll tell you where I've money hidden," I said. "You can say I surprised you and got away."

"Tell me where you have this money and I'll let you go," he answered at once. I could see the cunning smugness creep into his eyes as I seemed to innocently grab at his offer.

"Here, inside my shirt," I said. "A special pouch strapped under my left armpit." As I'd figured, he grabbed at the chance.

Falling to one knee, he leaned forward to reach inside my shirt, his breath stinking of fish and garlic. As his arm reached inside my shirt, I kicked out with my foot. The kick caught him right in the groin. His mouth flew open in a gasp of pain, and as he fell backwards he clutched at himself with both hands.

I was on my feet, bringing one shoe down hard on the side of his neck. His body stiffened, jerked twice and lay still. I saw the burst veins of his neck already coloring the skin of his jaw. I rolled him against the far wall with my foot and started for the door and the rusted hinge. Pressing the wrist bonds against it, I rubbed them along the jagged edge and felt them give in moments. My hands came apart, and I dived out of the doorway just as the other one came racing up from the beach.

I waited at the side of the doorway as he came bursting in, yelling in combined Arabic and French. I caught him with a fist to the stomach which doubled him up. A hard right uppercut deposited him across the room. I picked up one of the broken-down chairs and smashed it to pieces on his head. He lay crumpled, his skull bashed in, waiting for death to take over.

I picked up my paint box and checked the contents. Everything was there. I walked into the sunshine and down the road toward Casablanca. Glen Travis, painter of pictures, was on his way again but

the momentary interruption had had its educational
side. He had learned that it was wise, in this land,
never to get too far away from Nick Carter, Killmas-
ter, Agent N3.

The road ran along the shore and, though hot,
was scenic and direct. I saw turbaned men and
veiled women, farmers herding their small herds of
goats and sheep. At a village I passed through it was
obviously *souk*, market day.

Small clusters of merchants and farmers had set
up shop and were busily buying, selling and trading.
I paused to purchase some *kesrah*, the nourishing
Moroccan bread, from a veiled woman. It was warm
and I bit off pieces as I walked along. I saw clothing
that bore the influences of both Arab and western
styles.

As I saw the modern buildings of Casablanca rising on the horizon, and as I drew nearer to them I
noticed many more girls in blouses and slacks and a
few miniskirts, walking beside other women in the
traditional *haik* and I came to realize this was sym-
bolic of the city itself, the old and the new intermin-
gled, living side-by-side, often totally ignoring each
other.

I found the paint box to be almost a badge, and I
found myself receiving lingering glances, particu-
larly from the younger girls. I could see that the life
of an artist had certain very appealing characteristics, and I had to remind myself that the role was a
cover not a golden opportunity. I had other things
to pursue, namely one Anton Karminian, Exporter
and Importer.

Hawk's steel-blue eyes flashed in front of me, and

I could hear his voice as I trudged along the dusty road.

"Karminian's last message was that he'd gotten hold of something big," he had told me across the desk. "He wanted someone to make special contact with him for further information. Of course, that meant he wanted to bargain for some real money. But it also meant he was onto something. He'd never given us any phony leads."

"And that was the last you heard from him?" I had added.

"Right, Nick," Hawk went on. "He never made the next usual contact with us. He just vanished. Our tries at contacting him have all failed. I smell something has gone wrong. These old bones are creaking and that means trouble."

I had passed over the old bones bit. Hawk was one of the ageless ones. The "old bones" was a euphemism for one of the canniest noses for trouble on the planet Earth. Over and over I'd been involved in that personal sonar system he operated for AXE.

"That part of the world has been amazingly quiet for us," he had said. "Oh, the Israelis and the Arabs have been erupting on the other side of Africa and we know the Russians are all over, trying to stir up things, but Northwest Africa has been quiet. Morocco has almost been a Moslem Switzerland, a meeting place, a neutral area. In fact, the entire Mediterranean basin has been kept relatively quiet. And now, this. I don't like the feel of it."

Hawk's face faded away, and I thought of the task before me. Find the man Karminian, if he could be found. Maybe he was in hiding. Maybe he was dead. If I couldn't find him, try to find out what it was he had come onto and contacted Hawk about. A series of closed doors in a vacuum. A pursuit of questions wrapped up in a man known only by name.

I had reached the outskirts of the city, sauntering with a certain nonchalance. I walked down the Boulevard Moulay Abderhaman, past the port, the waterfront with its rows and rows of ships nudging each other in careless profusion. Tankers, freighters, passenger liners, ships from every land in the world, the spanking clean, newly painted ones and the rusted old veterans of a million pounding waves.

The waterfront, like all waterfronts everywhere, was a mountainous series of boxes, crates, barrels and bales. Casablanca, *Dar-el Beida* in Arabic. It was the Portuguese who had originally given the city its name of the White House in the 16th century, and I noted that the *medina*, the Arab quarter, that crowded, teeming, swarming mass of humanity, edged the harbor itself. I smiled inwardly as I wagered that a helluva lot of cargo quietly found its way into the bustling *souks* of the *medina*.

I turned from the waterfront to cross over the boulevard, down the Place Mohammed V to the Rue Quedj where, I'd been briefed, Karminian had his store. I found the place quickly enough, shuttered and locked. Going to the back, in a small areaway, I found a side doorway. Putting down my paint box, I tried the door. It held but moved slightly. The lock was a simple one and I had it open in minutes.

The store itself was cluttered with the vases, statuary, paintings and bric-a-brac of an importer of *objets d'art*. The place had the musty odor of a small area that has been closed for at least a week. It revealed nothing and I left the same way I'd entered, locking the door behind me.

We knew he had an apartment not far away, and it was my next stop. The building was a second-floor walk-up, an old, narrow place with the usual arched doorway.

The door to his apartment swung open gently as I knocked. I entered, carefully, and immediately saw the place had been ransacked. Clothes were pulled out all over, personal items scattered around, furniture overturned, dresser drawers emptied onto the floor.

I roamed through the three small rooms that made up the apartment. From the living room, one window looked down on the street. It seemed that I was not the only one looking for Karminian. But then, I had to remind myself, this mess could have been the result of an ordinary garden-variety robbery. It just could have been but I didn't buy it.

My own sixth sense told me differently and what I saw told me something else. If Karminian had left to go into hiding he had done so very quickly and taken almost none of his clothes.

Examining the lock, I saw that it hadn't been broken but only slipped. I closed the door and sat down, pushing aside a bundle of sheets, and thought about my next move. My decision was made for me by two items I found. One, lying on the floor beside an overturned dresser drawer, was a small address book. Inside there were only a few names, most of them other importers or buyers. But there was one name, "Athena," and a phone number alongside it. I made a mental note of both.

Then, beside an ash tray a book of matches leaped

out at me. "The Club Bedouin," they announced. "25 Rue du Kassim." I opened the matches and read the announcement on the inside cover. "Athena the Exotic," it read. "The Belle of Athens."

I left my paint box in the apartment, slipping two tubes of paint into my pocket, and headed for the Club Bedouin. I was much too early for the evening's festivities but I did get to talk with the bartender. He was helpful, confirming that Karminian was a frequent visitor at the club and a constant escort of Athena, the exotic dancer. Karminian, he said, was an extrovert, a gregarious sort. I told him I'd be back to see Athena and I wandered back to Karminian's apartment.

A thought was forming in my mind and I was warming to the idea fast. Instead of holing up in some hotel, why not stay at Karminian's apartment, I asked myself. With time to really go over the place, I might turn up some even better leads. And, even more intriguing, something could turn up of its own.

Making a fast decision, I spent the rest of the afternoon straightening up the place. By the time I was ready to return to the Club Bedouin, I had the place looking quite neat and presentable.

While the Club Bedouin wasn't exactly a dive, it wasn't very far from it. But I slipped on a necktie as a concession to their desire for dignity. I got a spot at the head of the bar with a good view of the small stage. I waited through two singers and a miserable magician whose best trick was to make himself disappear at the end of his act.

Then Athena came on in the usual swirl of veils that only partly hid a jeweled bra and sequinned panties. In the changing lights it was hard to really get a good look at her, and the heavy makeup didn't help much. But, as she started to shed veils it was plain that she had a firm, youthful body, a little too short-waisted to be really graceful, but with beautiful, round, high breasts.

I'd seen exotic dancers all over the world. The good belly dancers, when they weren't using their fancy name, had a natural sinuousness, a native grace. The rest all worked at it and never did more than that.

Athena, I quickly decided, was one of the latter. She did everything they all do, the sensuous posturings, the hip-shaking, the belly thrusting, the slidings, the simulated orgasms, all of it. But in my book she got A for effort and that was it. The natural ones established their claim within minutes. The others only established that they were imitators, some better than others, but still imitators.

But the crowd at the Club Bedouin were far from connoisseurs, and they drank in Athena's performance. Finally, sweating hard, and down to only bra and panties, she ended her dance and disappeared through a small door at the back of the stage. I left my drink, followed along the walls of the club and arrived backstage.

Backstage was a dingy, dreary hallway with an open door leading out into a back alley and a closed door off to the right. I knocked politely at the closed door and waited. In a few moments it was opened and Athena peered through the crack, suspiciously, cautiously. She was still in costume, but she had doffed the false eyelashes. Without them, and close up, she looked much younger and less the *femme fatale*, her eyes a soft blue.

"Yes?" she asked. "What you want?" She spoke in a heavy Greek accent.

"I want to talk with you for a few moments, if I may," I said for openers.

"About what?" she replied, suspicion instantly in her voice.

"About someone you know," I smiled, trying to put her at ease. "Anton Karminian."

"I don't know anything about heem," she shot back but I caught the flash of fear that had leaped into her eyes. She started to slam the door shut but I got a foot on the threshhold and held it open.

"Please," I said calmly. "I'm looking for him, and I thought you might help me."

"No, no," she said angrily. "I know nothing." She tried slamming the door again but my foot was still there. She tried pushing my foot with hers, but it wouldn't push. Suddenly she yanked the door open and leaned out.

"JIMMEEEE!" she yelled at the top of her voice. I turned and saw "Jimmeeee" emerge from the rear of the club, a big, beefy form with the rolling gait of an ex pug.

I'd met the type many times over. Every sleazy little joint had one as a bouncer. He didn't ask questions either, which was also typical of his kind. He just took in the scene, made his one-tracked conclusions and moved in.

I knew that even to attempt explanations would be a pure waste of time and breath. But I also knew that Athena was far too reluctant to talk about her friend, Karminian. I was going to find out why. I let Jimmy grab me by the collar and start to rush me out into the alleyway. I offered only token resistance.

"Cut it out," I said. "I only wanted to talk to her."

"Shut up, bum," he growled. I sighed silently. Everybody had to do their bit, including me. As we reached the alleyway, I braced my feet on the ground, tightened up and with a quick twist, had one thick arm in a judo hold. I twisted and he went sailing into the alleyway to land on both knees.

I saw the look of astonishment on his battered face as he started to get up. He was big and there was no doubt a fair amount of muscle still under the layer of lard he carried, but he was shamefully out of condition. In addition, I could see that he'd never had the reflexes to be anything but a third-rate pug. He moved at me, more carefully now, shot out a jab which I easily slipped. He tried another and I ducked away. He made little motions with his hands, did a small shuffle as a matter of habit, and tried two hard blows, a left and a right cross.

I blocked them and backed away. Then I feinted, starting off as though I were going to try and run past him. He lunged at me but I wasn't there. I'd ducked backwards and as his lunge carried him past me, I came up behind him, put my shoulder into his back and drove forward hard. He slammed into the wall and I heard the crack of his forehead against the bricks. I stepped back and he slumped slowly to the ground, like a burlap sack emptying out its contents.

I turned back to the club just in time to see the door to Athena's dressing room open and a flash of green disappearing down the corridor in the opposite direction. I ran and found another exit leading to another alleyway. I glimpsed the green coat racing around the corner and took after it.

She was heading for the park behind the Boulevard Rachidi when I caught up to her. I grabbed her wrist and spun her around. I was going to be soothing again, when I saw her hand come out of her purse and the glint on the blade of the pocketknife. Athena slashed at my hand holding her wrist and I let go quickly. She stood with the little knife held in front of her, her eyes mixed with fear and anger.

"Get away from me," she said in her strangely accented voice.

I shrugged, started to back off and for a moment I saw her relax. All I needed was that moment. I dived forward, grabbed her wrist and twisted, and the knife fell from her hand. She gasped in pain.

"Ow! Goddamn you," she cried out in pure Americanese. "Sonofabitch. Let me go."

"Well, well," I said, keeping my hold on her wrist. I had turned her around so that her back was against my chest and I held her arm pulled up behind her back. I looked down into her grimacing face. "What happened to Athena, the Belle of Athens?" I grinned.

"Let go of me, you bastard," she hissed. She brought her heel down hard along my ankle, raking my flesh with it.

I yelped, spun her around and grabbed her by the throat. There was a sudden terror in her eyes.

"You behave or I'll break you in little pieces," I growled. Athena had been around and she read the message in my eyes. "All I want is some answers," I added. "And I'm going to get them, sister."

"No rough stuff?" she asked fearfully.

"Not unless you force it," I answered. I let go of

her and she stepped back, her eyes combining resentment with respect.

She had, I noted, slipped on a silk minidress, a deep pink, and, I wagered, not taken the time for anything else. The small points of her nipples stood out deliciously beneath the silk, forming tiny, sharp mounds. Even without a bra she was high-busted and full.

"You're American," she said, interest creeping into her voice. "What do you want?"

"Just some information," I answered.

"That's what *they* said," she answered bitterly.

"They?" I questioned and she looked around nervously.

"Look, my place is only two blocks from here," she said. "If you want to talk let's go there. I'm not standing around here at this hour."

"Start walking," I said. I fell into step beside her and glanced down at her small, pretty face. Without the heavy makeup she had a face that once, I was sure, was sweetly pretty. It was still pretty enough, but a hardness had come into it. She wasn't much more than twenty-five, I guessed.

"Sure you can trust me enough to take me to your place?" I asked, somewhat maliciously.

She glanced up at me.

"No, I'm not sure," she said. "But I'll chance it. I figure maybe as an American you might take it easy. Besides, there's something different about you. You're not the usual bum around here, and you're not one of the tourists out for a cheap feel either."

"I'm an artist," I said. "A traveling painter. Since you're not from exotic Athens, where are you from?"

"I'm from exotic Akron, Ohio," she grunted. "I

know the next question by heart, mister. What am I doing here?"

"Good enough guess," I said. "What's the answer?"

"Nothing glamorous, I can tell you that," she said. "I was with a small troupe on tour. I met a guy here and got hooked on him. I stayed on with him when the troupe left. A little later, I found out that he never had any long-range plans for us. I found that out the morning after he cleared out, taking every cent I had with him."

"And you've never heard from him since," I supplied.

"How'd you guess?" she said bitterly. "I got a job at the Club Bedouin. It was the only place that would hire me without a permanent visa or a resident entertainer's license. They're not too fussy at the Club Bedouin, and it was a job and I was grateful. The old Turk that runs the place is all hands, but he's harmless. I've been trying to save enough to get out of here."

We had reached her place and she led me into a first-floor apartment, three rooms, but smaller than Karminian's flat and considerably more run-down.

Athena flung off her coat and I saw the nice, firm shape of her body. Her legs, a little short in the calf, were shapely and youthful and attractive. The pink dress clung to her and there was no faint line of even a pair of bikini panties. I was certain now about the bra by the way her full breasts moved beneath the silk, swinging freely and tantalizingly.

"What's your real name?" I asked.

"Aggie," she said quickly. "Aggie Foster. God, I haven't said it in so long it sounds funny to me."

"All right, Aggie," I said. "Where is your friend Karminian?"

I saw the suspicion leap into her eyes at once.

"I don't know," she said. "What do you want to know about Anton for? Who are you? I don't even know your name."

"I told you I'm an artist," I said. "My name's Glen, Glen Travis. Your friend Karminian bought a number of paintings from me through the mail, but he never paid me so I came down here to collect and found him gone. I want my money."

She studied me, her gutter-perception working overtime to decide about me.

"You can believe me," I said casually.

"I guess so," she finally said. "I've never known an artist before but you ain't exactly my idea of one. And you were handling Jimmy like a pro."

"I used to box," I said blandly. "I made money that way for my art lessons."

She sat down in a deep chair and her dress rose up to mid-thigh as she crossed her legs.

I was thinking that she was a hell of a lot sexier and really better looking offstage than on. But whether she completely believed my story was unimportant. I didn't swallow hers, yet.

"Where is Karminian?" I asked again. "I think you know."

The sudden concern in her eyes was very real as she answered.

"No, I don't, honest I don't," she said. "He just up and left. He told me he had to go unexpectedly, business, and that was the last I heard from him. I'm worried about him. Anton was the only nice thing that happened to me during the last year."

I decided that perhaps she was telling the truth. She wasn't clever enough to be that good a liar.

"You implied someone else was around asking for him," I said. "Who?"

"Four men," she said with a shiver. "Big bruisers with accents of some kind. They didn't believe me, and they said they'd be back for me unless I started remembering. They scared the hell out of me. I couldn't make them believe I didn't know anything."

I sat back and my mind was racing. It proved what I'd suspected. Karminian's apartment hadn't been ransacked by ordinary thieves. I had company in my search for him. But if I were going to track him down I'd need to know more about him.

Man, it was discovered long ago, is a creature of habit. Even in hiding, his basic behavioral pattern will emerge. He can change his hair, his name, his appearance and his friends but not his basic self. It was a truth known to every police force in the world.

"Your friend, Karminian," I asked casually. "What was he really like? A lot of people seem to want him very much."

I watched her eyes suddenly turn soft and sentimental and the hard edge of her face dissolved. In pensiveness, her youthful prettiness made a temporary comeback.

"What was Anton really like?" she mused aloud. "That's not hard. He was fun. He was fun when I needed fun and he was good to me. He liked to drink and he drank a lot, but he was never a sloppy drunk. We'd go out a couple of times a week after I'd finish at the club. We'd hit most of the all-night spots.

"Anton loved what he called *le jazz hot*. He'd

listen for hours to it and he taught me a lot. I remember how he'd listen to old records and point out little things to me, the importance of how Benny Goodman played a run, the way Louis Armstrong took a certain phrase. He taught me a lot. He even taught me enough French to get around here in Casablanca. He liked people and good times. I wish he'd get back."

I filed what she had told me in my mind. They were important bits of information. He was gregarious, a jazz buff and a big drinker, all habits which were bound to assert themselves.

"Who else might know more about him?" I asked. "He must have had other friends."

Athena leaned back in the chair, and her nipples pushed hard against the silk, forming twin pink points, unmistakably unconfined. She was seemingly unaware of the thrusting provocativeness of her breasts.

I forced my mind back to the subject we were discussing, Karminian, the disappearing importer.

"Look, honey," I said soothingly, "maybe he's in trouble. Maybe he needs help and that's why he disappeared. If I can track him down I'll let you know."

It was an unsubtle ploy but it hit home. She really felt for the guy, and her face reflected unconcealed anxiety.

"I know," she said. "That's what I keep thinking about. All right, go see Yussif ben Kashan, the rug dealer, in the Arab quarter. Anton used to talk about him often. And the bartender at the Chez Caliph on the Boulevard Zerktouni."

"Thanks, Athena," I said. "Or should I call you Aggie?"

She thought about it for a moment and then smiled. It was the first time she'd smiled since I met her, and there was a great sadness in it. "You use Aggie," she said. "Because you're American and because I haven't been called Aggie in a long time."

I stood up and drank in her compact little body, my eyes lingering on the sharp, upturned points of her breasts.

"I thought artists looked at girls differently," she said quietly.

"How do you mean 'differently?'" I asked grinning. I knew damned well what she meant.

"Differently," she repeated. "More like it didn't mean anything."

"Only when they're painting them, honey," I grinned. "And sometimes not even then. It always means something. We artists appreciate beauty. Beauty excites us even more than most people."

"Do I excite you?" she asked, the female conceit immediately leaping to the fore, the eternal female built-in need to be desirable.

"What do you think?" I countered. I felt like telling her I wanted very much to slam that firm little body down on the bed and explore its curves and hills, to see if that exotic dance act of hers could be translated into reality. But I held back as I saw the growing interest in her eyes. I wanted to keep it growing, for a while anyway.

Maybe she had told me all she knew about Karminian and maybe she hadn't. I wanted to find out. I was mildly surprised by her answer to my question, but then it was merely another facet of that same female need.

"Would you like to paint me?" she asked slyly, casting a sideways glance.

"Yes," I said. "Let's talk more about it tomorrow."

She nodded and her eyes were no longer suspicious and defensive. I was making fast headway with Aggie Foster. I hoped I could do as well in finding her boyfriend.

More and more I was becoming convinced that it wasn't going to be merely a question of finding him but a race as to who would find him first. Whatever Karminian had gotten hold of, that "something big" he'd contacted Hawk about, involved more people than I realized.

Aggie Foster watched me walk down the stairway and I knew she was already anticipating my next visit. That was always the best way to leave them, waiting, anticipating, intrigued.

# CHAPTER 2

I slept well after shoving a heavy table against the door as a precaution. In the morning I began to go over the apartment and Karminian's things with a fine-tooth comb, starting at one end of the place and painstakingly examining every inch.

My first surprise was his collection of records stacked alongside a small, portable record player, an American machine. From what Aggie Foster had told me about the man I expected a collection of good jazz, Muggsy Spanier, Pee Wee Russell, Buck Clayton, Goodman, Armstrong, Eddie Condon, the greats, at least.

Instead, the records were Bach, Mozart, Palestrina, Scarlatti and some Gregorian chants. Many of the record albums bore handwriting in a lovely, feminine script, small, brief messages: "Anton, just saw this and had to pick it up for you." Or, "Hope you like this." All were signed "Marina."

What the hell was a jazz buff, an avid fan of *le jazz hot* doing with a collection of classical records only, and the baroque classicists, at that? Naturally, I wondered who "Marina" was too. I also found a collection of pipes. Karminian was apparently a pipe-smoker and, like so many pipe-smokers, a mild collector of pipes. He also had a good stock of liquor in a cabinet and I fixed myself a good, cold martini for lunch.

The rest of the apartment turned up nothing I could determine as of importance. I decided to follow up some of the leads Aggie had given me, starting with Yussif ben Kashan, the rug dealer.

The *medina* or Arab quarter of Casablanca was a teeming, jostling, overcrowded, colorful place. It also smelled of too many people crowded into too little space, of a variety of foods being sold at hundreds of little stands. In the *medina* it seemed that every day was *souk* day, the market a continuous, bustling affair.

I threaded my way past robed women and tourists, *djellaba*-clothed men and those in western business suits. I passed a woman selling *harira*, hot soup being boiled in huge iron kettles and others cooking *mechoui*, a kind of Moroccan cookout of mutton grilled over hot embers.

Rugs, copper, brass, leather and glassware were hawked from hundreds of brightly colored little booths and tents. I was jostled, pushed and squeezed out of shape by the crowds at some spots and over everything was the din of voices raised in bargaining and arguing, the only accepted manner of doing business in Morocco.

I managed to ask around and learned that Yussif ben Kashan was not one of the itinerant merchants who came to the *medina*. He had a store, an establishment of permanence which I finally located. It was a wooden hole in the wall hung with colorful Moroccan carpets.

I saw those from the mountains of the Middle

Atlas woven in hues of beige, russet and brown. Those from the *Chicaqua* of the High Atlas range were of flaming scarlet and ochre and the Saharan rugs were muted reds, whites and blues. The linear designs and motifs were reminiscent of those of the South American Indians.

Yussif ben Kashan, I quickly learned, was not only a rug dealer but a human guidebook to the pleasures of the *medina*. He bowed as I entered, his *tarboosh*, the traditional red *fez*, dipping almost to the ground. He wore a *serwal* with *babouches* on his feet, the soft, ornately embroidered Moroccan slipper.

"*Salaam*," he said, his face soft and round and cherub-like. He sported a little pot belly to match. "You have come to gaze upon my beautiful rugs?"

"*Salaam*," I answered. "The rugs are indeed magnificent, but I come to Yussif ben Kashan for other reasons."

His small eyes narrowed for an instant and his round little face broke into a smile.

"Ah! You seek the pleasures of the *medina*," he oozed.

"Girls, of course. One? Or two? Or perhaps many? Perhaps eunuchs as soft and sweet as girls?"

I held up my hand to turn him off. "No, no," I interjected, finding a space in his rush of words. "I am looking for someone and I was told you might know of his whereabouts. I seek the man named Karminian."

"Karminian?" Yussif ben Kashan's eyes widened. "Oh, indeed I know him. He came to Yussif ben Kashan for many pleasures. He was a man of many sensual tastes, one of the greatest. He sometimes came with pretty women, sometimes alone but always to have me find the most unusual the quarter has to offer in the way of erotic delights."

And that, I said to myself, would be pretty damned unusual I'd wager. "Do you know where Karminian might be staying?" I asked, trying to sound more concerned than determined.

The rug dealer shrugged. "At the end of this street there is a right turn that ends at a small house in the center of a small *djenina*," he said. "Go there and speak to Fatasha the Berber woman. Karminian often spent days there."

The rug dealer paused and smiled, more to himself than to me. "With Fatasha, it is a place to spend days."

"*Soukran*," I said, thanking him. "I am indebted to your graciousness. I am staying at Karminian's apartment. If you hear anything more about him, please call me there. I will be happy to pay for good information."

I wrote the phone number on a scrap of paper which he carefully tucked into a trouser side pocket. In case I didn't uncover Karminian at this Berber woman's house, the bait of information money would attract ben Kashan, I was sure.

"May your search be successful," he said, bowing low as I went out the door.

"*Inch'Allah*," I answered, going out into the broiling sun again.

I followed the narrow street, pushing my way through hordes of people, turned right at the end and came to the small house set back in a small garden. The doorway was open and I stepped inside. It was cool and darkened with drawn blinds shutting out the sun. I stood still for a moment and was

CK-3

about to call out when from inside a draped archway, a woman stepped forth.

She was tall, wearing a jeweled bra and ballooned turkish trousers with ornate *babouches*. Loose, hanging black hair gave her high cheek-boned face a somewhat wild appearance. She had a prominent nose and wide mouth. Huge, bronzed earrings and a jewel in the center of her forehead added to her bizarre appearance. The jeweled bra strained to keep in huge, pendulous breasts.

Bizarre and wild as she appeared, there was an air of unvarnished, animal sensuality to the woman as she regarded me, hands on hips, with the quizzical stare of a woman for whom there are no more surprises.

"Salaam," I said. "Yussif ben Kashan sent me to see you."

A brilliant grin suddenly erupted and she showed a set of flashing, white teeth. Nodding for me to follow, she slipped through the curtained archway. I went on in and found myself surrounded instantly by a bevy of excited, chattering little girls.

I guessed they ranged from 11 to 14 years of age and they were completely naked, clustering around me, pushing and thrusting their nubile bodies forward. Their bodies were slender, light to dark brown and really very beautiful in their fresh, flowering loveliness, and I was reminded that the ancient Greeks thought a woman was at her most beautiful when she was 12 to 14, boyish and yet feminine, not immature and not mature.

I felt their hands on my body, running up and down my arms and legs, feeling the hardness of my muscled frame, and their chattering grew louder and more appreciative. Their pubescent, nymph-like beauty was enhanced by the unmistakable sensuality of their motions. One leaned back against a small table and spread her legs to apparently show me how close to virginal she was.

Fatasha was an erotic mother hen, grinning proudly.

"You like, aye?" she said. "They all yours. You have good time here at Fatasha's. You find these girls make you go very high."

"Hold it, hold it," I said. "I only came to ask you some questions."

"You ask questions?" She frowned, a dark cloud seemingly enveloping her face.

I thrust a dollar bill at her.

"Here, for your time," I said. "I look for the man Karminian. I was told he might be here at your house."

The money helped to assuage her hurt feelings at my turning down her choice offerings.

"Karminian is not here," she said a little gruffly.

"When did you last see him?"

"A week, maybe few days more," she answered. That helped to nail it down a little. He was around and alive as recently as a week ago.

I pressed again. "Did he tell you where he might be going?" I asked. "Did he tell any of your girls he was going away?"

Fatasha spoke sharply to the girls and they shook their heads. Once they realized I wasn't a customer they had sat down on a large bed and were busy talking, playing cards, and one even had a doll for which she was fashioning clothes, just as young girls anywhere would be doing. Only they were stark naked and serenely unconscious of it.

"Karminian not here," Fatasha said again, dismissing me with the phrase.

I nodded to her, slipped through the draped archway and went back into the heat of the streets. My next stop was the *Chez Caliph* and outside the *medina*, though the streets of Casablanca were busy with late afternoon traffic, they seemed almost empty to me.

I found the place on the Boulevard Zerktouni, just as Aggie had said, and the bartender was not at all reluctant to talk about Karminian. What he said, though, made my eyebrows go up, discreetly, of course.

"Sure, he came in all the time around five o'clock for a glass of sherry," the man said. He was a European who spoke English well. "Karminian was a loner, very quiet. He'd sit in a corner and just watch people. I only saw him with a woman once or twice, a gorgeous, black-haired dame, tall, real class."

That sure as hell wasn't Aggie Foster, I thought to myself. And Karminian a "loner?" That didn't fit either.

It was getting late and evening was already closing in. Without a good description of what the man looked like it was useless for me to try touring the jazz spots. I decided to go back to his apartment and wait there until it was time for Aggie to be finished, then visit her for a better description of the man.

I stopped in at a restaurant, the Rissani, and had a delicious meal of chicken cooked in olives and lemons and stuffed with almonds, raisins, semolina, honey and rice.

Back at Karminian's place, I was washing it all down with a nice long bourbon and water and thinking of how a man could be a gregarious, heavy-drinking patron of erotic pursuits and a sherry-sipping loner at the same time, a jazz buff with a record collection of Mozart and Scarlatti. Karminian was turning out to be a man of many parts.

I heard the sound of footsteps outside, clattering up the staircase, before I heard a woman's voice. The door suddenly resounded to short, hard knocking.

"Anton," the voice said, a low, mellifluous voice. "Let me in. I know you're there. I saw the light as I passed downstairs."

There was a pause and then some more knocking. "Anton," she said. "Please open up? What is it? What's the matter? Why did you come back without letting me know?"

I crossed to the door in two, fast strides and yanked it open.

The woman almost fell into the room and I caught her with my hand. Her eyes widened in astonishment and I took in gorgeous black hair, softly curled behind her ears, thin, black eyebrows over deep eyes of brown, delicately pronounced cheekbones and a rather long, aquiline nose. It was a face to remember, at once beautiful and proud, delicate and sensuous.

The body matched the face, full, thrusting breasts inside an off-white dress that clung like a petal to a flower. Her thighs curved in a long, slender line and somehow, I knew at once, who she was.

"You're not Anton," she gasped, finding her voice.

"No, but you're Marina," I said simply. "Come in, please."

She frowned and looked at me warily but entered the room. As I closed the door I saw that her breasts moved gently, provocatively as she walked, obviously held by a very loose brassière.

"Who are you?" she asked directly, fastening me with the deep, brown orbs that seemed to say more than her words.

"I'm Glen Travis," I said, smiling at her. "I'm looking for Anton Karminian and, since he's not here, I'm staying here. He owes me money for paintings of mine that he bought."

"How did you know my name?" she asked, her voice a low, sultry thing, velvet over fire.

"A guess," I said. "I saw the name on some of the record albums and you look as though your name would be Marina. It's a lovely name, an unusual name. It should go with a beautiful woman only."

"You know the right things to say," she smiled, and her lovely, proud face lighted with its own special glow.

"Most artists do," I said. "I want to find Karminian. From what you said, you may know where he is."

She sat down and a sadness crept into her eyes. "I wish I did," she said. "All I know is that Anton called me one afternoon and said he had to go away unexpectedly. He didn't even have time to see me to say goodbye."

"You were his girl friend?" I asked. She looked at me coolly.

"I was his friend," she said. "Anton and I had a very unusual relationship."

"I can believe that," I said. "You look the type who could have an unusual relationship. But you don't know where he went?"

She shook her head.

"You know," I went on, "it's very important that I

find him. I can't go into all the details, but if you help me you'd be doing him a big favor too."

"I cannot help you," she said, sitting down and crossing her legs. She wore only leg make-up, and the long line of her thigh was a thing of beauty.

I wished for a moment I really were artist enough to paint her.

"Marina," I said, turning the word over in my mouth. "An unusual name and an unusual girl, I would guess. Will you join me in a bourbon?"

"Scotch, please," she said. "On the rocks."

She settled back in the chair and studied me as I fixed the drink and handed it to her. Her breasts seemed to curve upward in a beautiful, graceful line as she sat relaxed in the chair.

"Having seen you," I said, "I think perhaps I don't want to find Karminian."

Marina smiled, a mischievous, slow smile that played around the edges of her finely molded lips. "But you do," she answered. "You want to find him very much."

"That's right," I said. "He owes me a lot of money."

"No," she said. "I think it is something more."

She was a smart dish, and I grinned at her. "Your special intuition," I said. "Some powers you have?"

"No, but there is something about you that makes me feel an urgency, perhaps even a sense of danger," she answered. "And yet, somehow, you make me feel as though I should help you, though I don't really believe your story about Anton owing you money for your paintings."

"Don't tell me you're an Egyptian fortuneteller," I laughed. She was too damned perceptive.

"I am part Spanish and part Moroccan," she said. "Maybe that does give me strange powers."

"Then you'd better believe me that your friend Anton might be in trouble if I don't find him," I answered. "I'm told he's a big drinker, and that can be dangerous."

"Anton? A big drinker?" she queried, frowning. "Absolutely not. Only wines, with perhaps a small brandy after dinner."

That fitted what the barkeep at the Chez Caliph had said. But nothing else fitted so far. "Tell me more about him?" I pressed.

"Anton and I, as I said, had an unusual relationship," Marina said, settling back deeper in the chair, her deep eyes growing distant and veiled. "He was very intellectual, very introverted. He never liked crowds or people in general. He preferred to stay here or at my place, just the two of us, quietly listening to records. He liked Bach, of course, and Mozart, but he had a special feeling for Palestrina."

"He smoked?" I asked, making my questions sound casual.

"Only his pipes," she answered.

"I was told he came on strong," I said and she frowned.

"What does that mean?" she asked genuinely.

I smiled.

"It means he was a sensual man, a lover of sexual pleasures, a big man with women," I answered.

Marina was frowning and her low, soft voice was almost indignant as she replied. "Ridiculous," she said. "He was an almost shy man, a man of the intellect not the body. That was the one . . ." She cut herself off and I grinned.

"Finish what you were going to say," I said. Her eyes narrowed.

"It was nothing," she answered.

"You were going to say it was the one missing thing in your relationship," I grinned.

She looked at me, her face set and beautifully composed. Only the flare of dark fire in her eyes told me I'd hit home.

"I hope I never get that intellectual," I grinned.

"You won't," she said with some asperity. "Anton could appreciate a woman's mind and sensitivity."

"So can I, honey," I said. "But not at the expense of ignoring the rest of her, and what you have just shouldn't be ignored."

She looked at me for a long moment and then laughed, a deep-throated, musical laugh, muted bells. "I could like you," she said. "You're so different from Anton."

I almost said that Anton was apparently pretty different all by himself, but she got up and started for the door.

She knew more than she'd revealed to me, I was certain, but that wasn't the only reason I didn't want her to go. Her eyes had held moments of hesitation, of holding back, and I wanted to know what she knew.

"Must you leave?" I said. "You're a very beautiful woman. I really wish you'd stay."

Her glance at me was veiled, but the veil didn't completely hide the interest in her eyes.

"Perhaps we'll be talking again," she said.

"You can count on it," I said. "And stop holding back. Help me find your friend Anton, and you'll be doing him a great favor."

She paused at the door and searched my eyes. "I

am at 9 Avenue Hassan Souktany," she said. "I will, as you Americans say, sleep on it."

I watched her walk off, her rear sinuously moving, ungirdled, inviting. I wondered, fleetingly, if beautiful women realized how easily they inflamed and excited and I knew the answer almost as soon as I'd had the thought. Yes. They knew it. They damned well knew it.

I closed the door and smiled to myself. Karminian had more than conflicting personalities; his taste in women was equally far apart.

I wondered if he were one of those men who assumed a completely different personality with different women, a man in whom different women brought out different things. I'd known that to happen, though not to such extremes as with Karminian. I also wondered if I were being lied to and by whom.

Aggie Foster's description of the man had been echoed by the rug dealer and by Fatasha with her nymphets. Marina and the barkeep at the Chez Caliph knew a very different Karminian.

The scream cut into my musings like a knife into soft butter. It was Marina's voice, the velvet cover torn off by terror.

I flung open the door, paused to grab two tubes of paint from my paint box, and raced down the flight of steps. I was just in time to see two burley men throw her into the back of a long, black Mercedes 600 Pullman limousine.

One shot a glance at me and I saw his square, crew-cut, thick-necked head, small blue eyes in a beefy face that might as well have been stamped MADE IN RUSSIA.

I also caught the glint of lamplight on blue

gun metal and I dove down and to the side. The slug tore past my head and into the wood of the doorway, sending big splinters flying. It must have been at least a .44 Magnum with a 240 grain slug.

I got up to see the big, black Mercedes 600 pull around the corner and I ran into the street and hailed a taxi.

"Follow him," I yelled, pointing to the twin dots of red disappearing around the corner. The cab was an old London Austin taxi and the driver a reluctant dragon. The Mercedes was pulling away fast and my man was more interested in keeping his *fez* on than really hitting it up.

"Pull over!" I yelled as we rounded a corner. He stopped, I ran out and yanked him from the driver's seat.

"*Moukkadem,*" I yelled at him which meant Government Agent, and I stepped on the throttle. "Allah will bless you," I tossed back at his surprised form sitting on the street.

I gunned the cab, putting my foot almost through the floorboards. I took the next turn on two wheels, invoking *Baraka*, divine protection. The Casablanca streets were fairly deserted at that hour and under my leaden foot the old taxi stayed with the Mercedes, at least. I really didn't want to gain anyway, preferring to stay back enough to just barely keep them in sight.

Finally, I saw the big, black car turn into a street and heard the sound of tires squealing to a halt. I pulled up alongside the curb and got out on the run. I stayed alongside a stone wall until I reached the corner and saw the Mercedes backing out. Only one man was inside it now, driving it away.

I let him pull off and then hurried to the entranceway of a typical, ornately decorated Moroccan house. I saw lights flicking on inside and looked around for a way in. It was easy enough. Low-hanging cross-bars formed part of the entranceway roof. I leaped up, caught an arm around one and pulled myself up onto a small rooftop.

A narrow ledge led to a large, arched window and I crawled along it, moving slowly on the precarious edge. The window opened easily at my touch and I crawled into the house, pausing inside to let my eyes grow accustomed to the darkness. The room was empty but through an open archway I saw lights and I heard voices from the floor below.

I moved on the balls of my feet, noiselessly, and was grateful for the tiled, Moroccan floor. I went through the archway into a corridor and now the voices were louder, angrier. I heard the sound of a slap followed by a short scream and then a long, pain-filled cry.

A flight of steps beckoned and I went down them, moving cautiously. Marina screamed again and I found myself on a narrow balcony that ran around the four sides of a room which looked down onto the room below it.

There, Marina was seated on a straight-backed chair, wearing only black panties and a loose black bra, surrounded by four Russians, one of them the crew-cut, beefy-faced man. Marina's breasts, upturned, full, magnificent, pushed forward as her hands were bound behind the back of the chair.

One of the Russians had a cattle prod, I saw, and he handed it to the crew-cut one.

"Here, Estan, you take it," he said.

Marina's head was forward and the one called Estan pulled her back by the hair roughly.

I saw the glistening shine of tears on her face.

"Where is Karminian?" the one called Estan asked, his accent rough and Russian. The other three carbon copies stood by, drinking in the girl's magnificence.

I felt my hands open and close, itching to get at their burly, stolid necks.

Marina, in bra and panties before these thugs, was like a precious painting before a herd of swine.

"Where is he?" the Russian shouted again. He pulled the girl's head back hard and I saw her breasts now fill the loose bra as she arched backward and cried out in pain.

"I don't know, I tell you," she gasped.

"Keep lying and we'll really start on you," Estan said. "You haven't seen anything yet." He drew back his arm and slapped her across the face with a tremendous blow.

Marina and the chair toppled over sideways and I heard her broken cry of pain.

"Why were you visiting his friend in the apartment?" the Russian shouted as the others picked up the girl and the chair together and set them upright on the floor again.

"I thought Anton was there," Marina gasped. "I thought he'd come back. I don't know the man who was there."

The Russian hit her again, not as hard this time but on her already bruised and reddened face it landed with even greater pain and the girl screamed again.

"You lie," the Russian said. "We have been watching the apartment. We saw the newcomer arrive and stay there. We'll get to him soon enough. It seems he also seeks Karminian and calls himself an artist."

The information one can pick up at keyholes, figuratively speaking, I said to myself. It was more than a little interesting to find out that the Russians were as anxious to get hold of Karminian as we were.

That meant one thing, anyway. If he were dead, they hadn't been the ones to put him out of business. And if he were only in hiding, was he hiding from the Russians or someone else? Karminian was taking on more intriguing aspects with every passing moment.

Marina's scream, ear-splitting and curdled with pain, stopped my musings and I looked down to see the Russian had thrust the cattle prod into her navel. He was getting more sadistic in his efforts to get information which Marina didn't have to give.

We artists hate to see beauty desecrated, I reminded myself, taking one of the two tubes of paint out of my pants pocket.

The balcony led to a narrow flight of stone steps at the far corner of the four-sided overhanging ledge. I unscrewed the cap of the tube and began to squeeze the paint, cerulean blue, along the balcony floor, next to the low side wall.

I worked my way back to the narrow stone steps until I had a long, thin trail of blue paint along one wall of the balcony. The paint was legitimate, acrylic-based colors that any artist could paint with, but Special Effects had also invested them with a secret ingredient.

I moved down onto the first few steps, took out my lighter and ignited one end of the long trail of paint. It began to sputter. It would flare for an instant and then explode. Because of the length of the trail, the explosion wouldn't be concentrated but still would be strong enough to do what I wanted, which was mainly to create an uproar.

I was at the bottom of the steps, diving into the corner of an L-shaped hallway, out of sight just beyond the door leading to the room where they were with Marina.

The paint exploded and I heard the crash of tile and stones as it did a good enough job apparently of jarring one side of the balcony loose.

The Russians came charging out of the room, shouting instructions at each other. Two of them went dashing into the house, a third started up the stairway. The fourth, the crew-cut one, halted and glanced around suspiciously. A pall of smoke and dust was beginning to roll down from the stairway to the balcony.

I came out of my corner full speed, Hugo in my hand.

The Russian saw me, saw the stiletto in my hand and kicked out with a speed and accuracy that caught me by surprise. His shoe hit my forearm, sending numbing waves of pain up to my shoulder.

I felt Hugo drop from my fingers.

The Russian made his mistake then. He dived for the stiletto. My own foot caught him at the side of the neck. I saw him grab at his neck, fall forward and grow red as he gasped for breath. I could have given him another that would have killed him but every second counted. He'd be more than minutes just trying to find enough breath for action.

I scooped up Hugo, my arm still numb, and ran into the room. Using the blade with my left hand, I shredded the wrist ropes and saw the utter astonishment in Marina's eyes.

"Grab your dress," I said.

She reached down and picked it up from the floor. Holding her hand, I headed for the doorway. I heard shouts. The others would be coming down from the balcony in moments. A window had shattered and using my foot to open up a larger hole, we leaped through it and out into the street.

Marina was struggling into her dress on the run. She had just got it on when I yanked her down. "Stay low," I hissed. We crawled forward along a low stone parapet behind a wall until we reached the corner.

I heard the shouts from the building, heard the sounds of running footsteps. By now they had discovered Marina was gone and were out beating the bushes.

I dropped from the parapet at the corner and reached up to help Marina down when the spotlight turned on, sweeping quickly over the street. It would be on us in minutes and I saw it was a hand-operated job, held by someone standing atop the same parapet we had crawled along.

I couldn't see the figure behind the glare of the battery powered light but I drew a bead on the spot and fired. It went dark in a clinking of shattered glass.

The old taxi was still there, and we ran for it.

"Get inside," I told Marina. "I'm chauffeur." I backed the cab around and sped off. I knew the big, black Mercedes would be coming out searching in minutes, but we'd be safely away by then.

"Where to, lady?" I said cheerily.

"I . . . I don't know," she said. "I'm still shaking."

"I'd go back to your friend Karminian's place but I'm almost certain they'll come looking for us there. Do you think they know where you live?"

"No," she answered. "They were watching Karminian's apartment, not mine."

"Then it's 9 Avenue Hassan Souktany," I said.

We were there in no time and I parked the taxi a few blocks from her building. It, too, was a walk-up, but more graceful and larger than Karminian's and a palace compared to where Aggie Foster lived.

Marina opened the door, and I walked into a living room richly draped in gold and black. A long curved sofa curled around one end of the room, and its black fabric contrasted with the plethora of brightly colored pillows of all sizes and shapes. I looked down to see Marina beside me, gazing up at me.

"Thank you for what you did," she said. "Excuse me for a moment, and then we can talk about it. I feel dirty and unclean. Make yourself comfortable. In the cabinet there is liquor. Please help yourself."

She disappeared into an adjoining room, and in moments I heard the sounds of running water.

I fixed a bourbon on the rocks for myself and a Scotch for her and sat down amongst the luxurious, bright pillows. I was sipping my drink when I looked up to see her standing in the doorway, a deep gold robe of silk reaching in a straight line to the floor, dropping from the high points of her breasts. Her hair hung loose below her shoulders and as she walked toward me, I saw her full, upturned breasts move easily and freely beneath the silk robe.

Marina turned down the large overhead light and the softer glow enveloped her delicate, high cheekbones in deepened shadows, heightening the regal, aristocratic bearing of her face. She picked up her Scotch, took a deep pull of it as she stood before me, and then folded herself alongside me, sinking into a pile of cushions.

Somehow, the silk robe never came open, never shifted to show an inch of her body. Only the loose movement of her breasts revealed that she wore nothing beneath the silk.

"Who were those men?" she asked quietly. "They were Russian, I know. Why did they want Anton?"

"I don't know." I shrugged. "Maybe he owes them money too."

She smiled.

"Glen," she said, "that is your story, but I do not believe it. Now I know something else is involved. I wish I knew more. Perhaps then I could help you. And Anton."

"And Anton," I said. "Let's not forget Anton. You just tell me where you think I might find him and you'll be helping us both."

She said nothing but her dark, deep orbs studied me. She watched as my gaze traveled around the opulence, the soft sensuality of the room and then paused to linger on her.

"So this is where you had intellectual evenings with Anton?" I mused aloud. I caught the slow smile that played about her lips.

"A waste, to your way of thinking, right?" she smiled. "Why? Lovely surroundings are just as important in the enjoyment of intellectual pursuits."

"Never said they weren't," I answered. "But I don't separate the mind and the body. I've never been an 'either/or' man. I can enjoy your mind as well as your body and vice versa. I don't believe in taking one or the other. I want 'em both."

"You're greedy." she laughed and leaned back.

For the first time the robe came open to reveal the

soft swell of her breast, a tantalizing mound for exploring.

I felt my hand move forward involuntarily.

Marina's eyes were deep, almost black, glistening orbs.

"Maybe I am," I agreed. "Don't tell me he never was greedy."

"Never," she said. "I told you, we had a very unusual relationship. I often wondered how I could remain so cool and platonic with Anton. I know now that it was he who kept it that way. He made love to me in his own way, with his mind, with music and poetry, with the soft touch of his hand on mine. He never went further than that."

I kept thinking of Karminian the big drinker, the patron of Fatasha, the devotee of strange and weird sexual pleasures in the *medina*. This was one hell of a strange cookie, this Karminian.

"You say, you know now that it was Anton who kept it on this level," I questioned. "Why do you know that now?"

"Because just sitting here I can see it would be impossible with you," she answered, her eyes twin black coals, glowing with a dark fire.

"You are damned right," I said.

I leaned forward, took the silk robe at the collar and pulled her to me. I saw her lips part as my mouth moved onto hers, and then I was tasting the sweet honey of her tongue.

She let it play with mine, then withdraw and then come forth again, inviting, tantalizing. Her breath had increased, and now her arms were sliding around my neck.

I felt my hand move onto the soft, smooth skin of her shoulders, my thumb gently pressing in, kneading the skin just beneath her shoulder bones. She tore her lips away and her cheek was against mine.

"No . . . no," she gasped. "I . . . I had forgotten how much I longed for this. But I cannot . . . no, please."

I moved my hands down an inch closer to her breasts and heard her draw her breath in sharply. "Why not?" I asked. "Being faithful?"

"Maybe," she whispered and looked up at me, her eyes asking for understanding.

But, a long time ago, I had learned that understanding is not always compassionate.

"Maybe that's it," she said. "Being faithful."

"To what?" I asked brutally.

I saw the shocked pain flare in her eyes and I reached into the silk robe and seized both lovely, full, pear-shaped breasts.

Marina cried out in anguished ecstasy and threw her head back, eyes closed, still trailing the remnants of her cry into the silent room.

"To what?" I repeated again and rubbed my thumbs over the soft, hardly protruding nipples.

Marina cried out again in half-anguish, half-rapture. It was her last such cry. She reached up and seized my neck, pulling my face down to bury it in her breasts.

I took her breast in my mouth and gently caressed its softness, moving it back and forth under my tongue until Marina was clutching at my back, my shoulders, my neck in a frenzy of desire.

I gently pulled away from her breasts as she gasped in delicious rapture. I took my clothes off slowly, watching her as I did, knowing she gazed at me through half-slit eyes and then, suddenly, she leaped forward to clasp my naked body to her, pressing her face against my abdomen, kissing me with feverish anxiety.

Here was a creature of passion who, in some strange, inverted way, had been able to hold off the roaring volcano that was within her. I was happy to be around for the eruption.

Marina's long-legged body slid beneath mine, one of the brightly colored pillows supporting the small of her back. She clasped her smooth thighs around my waist and welcomed me with a biting cry of pleasure, a gasp of unsuppressed joy, a cry of desire set free at last.

She moved beneath me, setting her own frenzied rhythm, and I felt the tips of her breasts enlarge and rise up in hunger.

My lips eagerly sought their softness, my tongue tracing gentle paths of pleasure around each eager circle as Marina moaned and murmured and whispered wild words of desire into the night.

Suddenly, I moved from her and for a split second she lay still, her gorgeous body held in suspended animation, and then she exploded against me in a frenzy of hungry passion.

"Oh, no, no," she gasped. "Oh, God, you can't stop . . . oh, no."

She grabbed at me, pulling me over her, writhing her hips feverishly, and now she was crying little sobs.

When I returned to her she screamed in a glorious mixture of relief and desire, and her hunger was insatiable.

Her mouth found my lips, my chest, as she arched her back, thrusting upward in her feverish desire to enjoy every possible part of me.

I stayed with her this time, moving faster and

faster until there were only mountain peaks, each one a little higher than the preceding one, and Marina gasped and cried out in overwhelming pleasure.

I felt her suddenly stiffen, her body grow tight around me and though her lips opened wide there was no sound from her and her deep eyes were in some other world all her own.

Only the quivering stiffness of her body told me what was happening and then, finally, she sighed, a long drawn sigh from the very depths of her innermost being, and she lay there, a limp, spent rag doll, a beautiful rag doll.

I moved beside her, laid my lips against one lovely, upturned breast, and she cradled my head against her.

"It's been too long," she whispered, hardly breathing. "And you knew. Somehow, you knew."

I didn't answer. I didn't know the answer, not for certain. Had I known, had I sensed her desires, her needs, in some subconscious way? Or had it been the reverse? Had she sensed, in me, someone with whom all that had been held back could be released?

It had then, for her, been both a surrender and a victory. It was that victory she spoke of later, when she held me close.

"We know so little about each other," she said. "But this had to be. I knew that from the moment we met."

Her victory, for her, had been complete but her surrender was equally so, and I knew it in the deep softness of her eyes.

I moved quickly, almost brutally so, knowing that she could no longer hold back.

"Where is Karminian?" I asked softly.

She just shook her head helplessly.

"All right," I pressed. "Who might know where he is?"

She spoke with her eyes closed, held tightly shut, as though she didn't want to hear her own words. "There is a man," she said, "called Rashid the Rif. He lives in the Arab quarter. Anton spoke of having important dealings with him."

I pressed my lips against one soft, pear-shaped breast.

"It is good you have told me, Marina," I said, breathing softly against the pink tip. "Believe me."

She stirred and lifted my head with her hands, gazing deeply into my eyes. "Who are you?" she asked, almost pleadingly.

"A friend," I answered.

It was true, as far as it went. I would be a friend, and a good friend, so long as it did not conflict with my mission. Friendship, in this business, like love, had its clearly defined limits.

# CHAPTER 3

Marina had made me promise to return soon. It was a promise she needn't have extracted. I had to push thoughts of her out of my mind.

The memory of her milk-white skin against the blackness of her hair, her beautifully formed breasts, her long, slender thighs, lingered in my mind, distracting, bothersome visions. Her hunger, so long denied, had not been satisfied this one time, I knew.

It was an exciting prospect to contemplate, but now I had other matters, ugly, dangerous matters.

Rashid the Rif, she had told me, and I headed for the little rug dealer in the *medina*. He would, I knew, be able to tell me where I could find this Rashid the Rif.

I searched my memory for what I knew of the Rifs. Little, long-buried facts began to sift their way up into my conscious mind.

The Rif was the fortress of Morocco, the mountainous stretch of inhospitable land in North Africa, from the tip of Morocco where it faces Spain, along the Mediterranean, to the Algerian border.

As conqueror after conqueror found out, the people of the Rif were fierce fighters, quick to anger, feeling themselves more than a little apart from the rest of their countrymen. The Romans could never conquer or subdue the Rifs in their natural stronghold. Neither could the Spaniards nor the French. The only Berber or Arab chiefs who made headway among the Rifs were those who came in peace and not to conquer.

The mountainous Rifs in 1926, under Abd-el-Krim, fought 325,000 French troops and 100,000 Spanish troops to a standstill with 20,000 men. Great horsemen, at home with their fleet stallions or the *mehari*, the sand-colored fast camels used on the desert ranges, the Rifs were a warrior caste, a proud, aloof people.

I wondered if that meant anything or whether this Rashid the Rif was merely a loner.

Ben Kashan didn't give me any leads on that. When he saw me he brought out a wan, apologetic smile.

"The sellers of information have become terribly greedy," he said, spreading his hands out wide, his eyes a mirror of concern.

I got the message.

"Tell the greedy ones that if the information they have is good, I will double what I would have paid," I answered. "Right now I come seeking one called Rashid the Rif."

Ben Kashan's face clouded and his eyes grew wary.

"He will tell you nothing," he said. "He is a bad man, a man to keep away from."

Ben Kashan's advice was sincere, but I knew that the Arabs in general disliked and feared the Rifs in a legendary fear going back a thousand years.

Ben Kashan saw in my eyes that I wasn't impressed.

"If you must find him, his house is on the other side of the *medina,* behind the row of gift stores. It was a stable once, his house."

"What does he do, this Rashid the Rif?" I asked.

Ben Kashan shrugged and rolled his eyes. "He is a Rif," he said. "He tells no one anything, he speaks to no one. He came to the *medina* only a few months ago and, I have heard, paid to rent this old stable. More than this, I do not know."

"Good enough," I said, tossing an American dollar at him. The part about only arriving a few months ago was interesting.

I found my way back across the *medina* and located the line of semi-permanent gift shops aimed at tourist trades, full of carpets, brass and copper utensils, and general native arts and crafts. Behind the row of shops I found the old stable. A low house, it jutted out in an L-shaped form.

I entered the open door and paused to pull on a bell rope just inside the doorway.

Rashid the Rif appeared from within the house silently, suddenly standing before me, unmistakably the man I sought. Wearing a *djellaba* with a cartridge belt slung around one shoulder and a long, curved Moorish dagger hanging from his belt, he regarded me with the eyes of a falcon, cold, piercing, predatory, deadly.

His face itself was hawk-like, sharp-nosed, with tightly drawn skin and a glance that skewered me as though I were a piece of mutton on a spit. The man fairly stank of evil and I felt the hairs on the back of my neck go up. He outwaited me as I spoke first.

"I seek a man called Karminian," I said. "I was told he visited you recently."

"I know of no such man, foreigner," he spat out, each word distinct in heavily accented Arabic.

"I was told he had business dealings with you," I tried again.

"If so, it was his business and mine, not yours," Rashid the Rif growled. "But I told you I know no such man."

I felt certain, without a shred of evidence, that he was lying. Besides, my own stubbornness was coming to the fore.

"I was told that he came to you only a week ago," I persisted. I watched, my eyes narrowing, as his hand went to the hilt of the long, curved Moorish dagger in its jewel-encrusted sheath.

"You say Rashid lies?" he muttered darkly.

"I say what I was told," I answered. I could feel myself getting mean, hoping the ugly bastard would try to use that curved pig-sticker on me. But he didn't, though I had the strong feeling that he wasn't putting aside the thought but merely deferring it.

"Too many questions is the way to lose one's tongue," he growled.

"Thanks," I said. "I'll have that tattooed on my chest."

I turned and strode out, knowing any further attempts at information would be futile. I felt the Rif's eyes following me until I was lost in the throng and when I emerged from the *medina* I took a deep breath.

It was becoming clearer that so far I had but two avenues to Karminian, both female. And I felt that both could be of greater help. I didn't think they were deliberately holding back, not any longer, but they could know little things which seemed unimportant to them but might be really important as hell to me.

I decided to go over that scene again, starting this time with Aggie Foster.

She had just gotten up a few minutes before I arrived and greeted me wearing bright-green, halter-top, bare-midriffed pajamas. She quickly covered the flash of pleasure in her eyes with a half-pout. Without make-up, she looked surprisingly little-girl, the hard, jaded lines of her face softened by the natural glow of her complexion.

"I was wondering what happened to you," she said, her lips thrust out in a pout. "I guess you're not that interested in finding Anton."

"Oh, but I am," I said, grinning at her. "I've been busy looking for him."

"I thought I'd hear from you yesterday," she said. "How do you know I didn't think of something?"

This time I grinned inwardly. It was a transparent ploy to see me but I wasn't going to stomp on it.

"Have you thought of something?" I asked quickly. "Let's hear it."

"No matter," she said, brightening up suddenly. "I wanted to see you on something else anyway. I've been thinking. A painting of me might be great publicity, something different from the usual glossy photos. Could you do something real sexy?"

"I don't know," I answered with a slow smile. "An artist can't just make up sexiness. It's something that has to come from his subject."

"It'll come," she said grimly. "Especially these days."

"Why especially these days?" I asked innocently. "You miss Karminian that much?"

Her eyes narrowed and she grew stiff, defensive. "What if I do?" she said, flouncing down on the small sofa, resting her arms on the back so that her breasts thrust forward, round, high mounds of inviting loveliness. Her foot moved back and forth, twitching restlessly, like a cat's tail.

I was here to get more on Karminian from her, but I suddenly saw a better route to what I wanted, certainly one that might be more fun.

"What did you think of that was important about Karminian?" I asked. "Apparently you've been thinking a lot about him."

She got the dig. "Maybe I don't feel like talking about it now," she answered quickly. "Maybe I forgot again."

"Like hell you did," I said, moving to stand in front of her.

She was being surly again, her restless eyes moving across my face.

I reached down, took the halter top in one hand and pulled her to her feet.

Instantly, her eyes showed fear.

"You promised no rough stuff," she said.

"Who said anything about rough stuff?" I asked. "I want to help your memory along. Maybe reminding you of him will do it."

I leaned down and kissed her, opening her lips with my tongue.

She didn't move her body but her lips worked against mine, responding at once.

"Is that what you miss?" I murmured, not taking my lips from hers, still holding her by the front of the halter.

"Bastard," she murmured back.

I let my tongue reach deep down into her, flicking back and forth, and I felt her body quiver.

"How's the memory?" I breathed, still holding my mouth on hers. "Getting better?"

"Bastard!" she said, trying to tear away but clutching at me at the same time. "Stop it. That's not fair."

I let my hands drop down to press across the halter and rest on her two high, round breasts.

She threw her head back and a half-sobbing cry escaped her. Her hands still clutched at my arms.

"Do you remember being held this way?" I asked. "Remember?"

"Oh, Christ!" she cried. "Cut it out. I can't stand it. Stop playing with me this way."

I stopped playing with her. I slid my hand under the halter to seize one softly firm, young breast.

Aggie almost screamed and threw her body against me. Her hips were making round motions, churning against my groin. She reached back and undid the halter top and it fell off to free my hand around her breast.

I ran my thumb across the small, pink, almost recessed tip, and she began to feverishly rub her body up and down against mine. Her breasts were indeed round and full and very youthful, and she pressed them into my hands, and her mouth against my neck was taking small bites.

I held her back for a moment and looked at her straining face, eyes tightly shut. She was nearly mad with desire, this unsubtle, simple little creature, delirious with unbridled, naked, raw desire.

I thought of how Marina, too, had been a creature of raw desire.

One was overheated from not having, the other from having. For a fleeting moment I found myself admiring this Karminian. In his own way, he was playing quite a game.

But then Aggie's fervid desire shut all else out. Her shoulders were moving in a circular, rotating motion and I felt her breasts grinding into my palms, her hips moving against my stomach.

I was experiencing a close-up version of her dance. I reached down, put one arm between her legs and lifted her from the floor to carry her into the bedroom.

She had the pajama bottoms nearly off by the time I put her down on the bed and as she tossed and writhed I took in her firm, young, full figure. She was compact, and every motion of her body implored, begged, entreated.

I undressed and laid my chest atop hers.

Aggie began to twist and turn and moan, small, happy sounds coming from her lips, more than gasps and not quite words. Unlike Marina, there was nothing languorous, nothing subtle, nothing refined about Aggie Foster's lovemaking. The exotic dancer was still basically a Midwest, small-town girl, and her lovemaking was blunt, a driving, uncontrollable force.

Aggie clutched me to her and rolled over atop me, her firm, compact body pumping and thrusting and driving.

I seized her shoulders and began to match the harsh, demanding movements.

She flung herself backward and cried out for me to do more. She didn't want brutality, and masochism wasn't part of her. She was merely totally caught up in raw passion.

As I made love to her, Aggie lifted her torso from the bed with each driving thrust, higher and higher, astonishing me with the strength of her small form. As I matched her every pushing, pumping movement, she cried out for more until suddenly she almost leaped into the air and clasped me to her with a wriggling, hip-grinding cry of ecstasy, and it was over and done with.

We lay side by side with only the bittersweet ecstasy left, the almost painful sensitivity of two spent bodies.

After a while, Aggie raised her head and I saw her eyes begin to focus, to return to earth as it were, and she looked at me as if coming out of a dream, her voice strained, hoarse.

"Christ," she breathed. "Oh, Christ, I'd never have believed it. I didn't think anyone could be better than Anton."

"You shouldn't make comparisons," I chided.

"I'm not," she breathed, resting her cheek on my chest. "I'm just saying what's true."

Once again, as I had with Marina, I didn't hesitate to take advantage of her warm, unguarded mood, of this brief period when she was emotionally my captive.

"Did you ever hear him mention someone called Rashid the Rif?" I asked softly. I saw her head nod.

"Just before he disappeared," she answered. "He told me he was afraid of someone called Rashid."

I grimaced to myself. The old bastard had lied, as I felt certain he had.

"Did Karminian take you to his apartment often?" I asked, tossing out another one.

The whole thing was being made up of unexplainable bits and pieces. It was becoming a game of how many more contradictions I could uncover.

"Never," Aggie murmured. "We either came here or went out."

"He smoked, didn't he?" I asked.

"Yes," she said. "Horrible, strong Turkish cigarettes. Nothing else but and he chain-smoked them."

Contradictions, contradictions and more of the same. I let Aggie cling to me a few minutes longer and then I moved out from beneath her. I had to get away and review this puzzle of contrasts but first I was going to pay another visit to Rashid the Rif.

Karminian had dealt with him and recently. It was the one solid bit of information I had, confirmed by both Marina and Aggie.

This time Rashid would talk. I looked forward to another meeting with the evil, falcon-eyed Rif.

"You'll come back, won't you?" Aggie said as I finished putting on my clothes. "I meant that about wanting you to paint me."

"Of course," I said, taking in the compact, earthy sexiness of her body as she lay looking up at me. "I'll stop by after you get back from the club . . . or perhaps just before you go. I'll see you."

"I like you," she said unexpectedly. "I mean, I think you're a nice person."

I smiled down at her.

The remark was so like her, simple, direct, uncomplicated. I put one hand upon her round breast and she held it there. I suddenly felt very sorry for Aggie Foster. She ought to have been back in Akron, Ohio, bedding down with some nice, simple, uncomplicated guy.

"I'll be back," I promised, and she let my hand go and turned over to snooze some more.

I left her that way and started down the street. It would be dark before I reached the *medina,* but I didn't hurry.

I was deep in thought, trying to unravel a mystery called Karminian, a paragon of contradictions, a split personality to end all split personalities. What solid information I'd uncovered only served to make the overall picture of the man more puzzling. But it wasn't just that, merely puzzling, I realized. The whole damned thing was somehow out of shape, a picture out of focus.

Aggie Foster described a man who was a wild swinger, a big drinker, an extrovert who loved crowds.

Marina told of a shy man who hardly ever drank, an introvert who hated crowds.

Aggie knew a jazz nut who knew the styles and habits of all the jazz greats, a real jazz buff who could dig it for hours.

Marina knew a lover of Scarlatti and Palestrina and poetry.

With Aggie he smoked only strong, Turkish cigarettes.

With Marina, never anything but his pipes.

One girl he took to his apartment frequently, the other he never brought there.

According to Fatasha in the *medina* he was a regular patron of far-out sexual pleasures, a connoisseur of the erotic.

To the barkeep at the *Chez Caliph* he was hardly ever seen with women.

And one more fascinating item kept rolling around in my head. Karminian had been an AXE contact man for years but the Russians were here, trying as desperately as I was to find him. Of course, this could be because they'd found out he had something on them but somehow, in the back of my mind, that didn't seem to hold water.

I went over the list quickly again and once more told myself that these were more than just contradictions.

Of course, I'd known people who were split personalities, contradictions within themselves. Such people were indeed studies in contrasts, their surface traits often directly opposed to each other.

Karminian could have been one such person. Or, he might have deliberately given himself two totally different personalities, one for Marina and one for Aggie. But right there is where I had to stop, where I couldn't take it any further.

A man could, for his own reasons, give himself two faces for different people. He could actually have a personality split very deeply but even a split personality only splits so far. If the guy were really a devotee of weird and wild sex, as both ben Kashan and Fatasha testified, I'd be damned if I could see him sitting around with something like Marina and holding her hand. It just didn't add up. And, conversely, if he was an ascetic, a strange duck who took his sex intellectually, vicariously, then I couldn't see him inside Fatasha's house of pleasure.

I just couldn't see anybody's split personality splitting that far. And yet, I had to admit that the sonofabitch seemed to have done it. It was my assignment to find him, or find out what had happened to him. But it had become more than an assignment.

Karminian had become a minor obsession with me. The man had become a figure of fascination and, in a way, admiration. He was leading two lives and doing the damnedest job at it too.

As I reached the *medina,* I put aside all thoughts of how he did it or why he did it.

Even at night, the Arab quarter was a busy, hustling place but in the dark it took on an added dimension.

The narrow, twisting, cobbled streets looked ominous, each of them, and the small, yellow lamps on the outsides of the houses added an eerie, shadowy glow to the place. The cry of the *muezzin* had given way to the soft, sensuous sounds of reed instruments, and, here and there, a prostitute's voice raised in a strange sing-song cry, not quite a call and not quite a song.

I passed the small shops, now closed and shuttered, their gifts put away for the night. I rounded the corner of a winding street that led to the old stable where I'd met Rashid and halted abruptly. Rashid had company.

Five horses were tethered outside the house, five pure-blooded Arabian stallions, unmistakable to anyone who knew horses by the sturdy, broad back, the high tail and large upper head with the added brain capacity, the slight bulge over the forehead called the *jibbah* by the Arabs.

I decided to circle around to the side of the house where a small, arched window beckoned invitingly some three feet over my head. I glanced around the narrow passageway and saw I was alone. I leaped, got a hold on the ledge and pulled myself up.

The window was open and I moved silently into what once must have been a grain or oats storage room. Four narrow crossbeams ran from the wall with the window across to the opposite wall where the door to the adjoining room stood open, the light streaming into the dark storage room.

I heard the sound of voices from the adjoining room, voices raised in angry urgency.

One of the narrow beams, the nearest one to me, ran to the top of the doorway. I edged my way out on it, keeping a precarious balance, inching my way across the narrow piece of wood. It was slow going, and I took a few painful slivers of dry wood in the belly, stopping each time to pull them out.

Finally I reached the end of the beam where it met the wooden lintel across the open door. The lintel had a small, curved space above it and through it I peered down at a room where the five Rifs stood around a small table with Rashid.

A sixth man, his back to me, wore trousers, a shirt and a small, high peaked cap. The others were all wearing their *djellabas* and, like Rashid, decked out in cartridge belts, pistols and the curved Moorish daggers.

The Rifs, I knew, spoke a Berber dialect called *tarrafit* and I thanked the Lord they weren't using it. They were speaking French, a choice dictated by the presence of the sixth man in western clothes, I presumed. One of the Rifs, taller than the others, was arguing with Rashid, whose piercing eyes were glittering in anger.

"Karminian is dead," Rashid was saying. "I killed him myself, I tell you."

I almost lost my balance at that one. It appeared I had at least some of my answers at last.

"Then why do so many seek him?" the tall Rif asked. "They do not think him dead."

"They do not know it," Rashid argued. "But they will not find him. He is done with."

"So you say, my brother," the tall Rif answered. "But El Ahmid knows that if the jackals stir up enough dust, the vultures will be attracted. We cannot take chances, not now."

The sixth man spoke.

I wished I could get a look at his face.

"Indeed we cannot," he agreed. "Things have been put in motion. It is too late to stop now or to have something go wrong now. My people would be terribly upset if something went wrong now."

"Nothing will go wrong," the tall one answered. "It is a long ride from the Casbah at Tangiers but we have come here to eliminate the jackals. They will join the one they seek, each one of them. That way we will be rid of them all, and there'll be no more questions and attempts to find Karminian."

He turned to Rashid. "You do not argue the wisdom of El Ahmid's decision, I hope," the tall one said. "I can tell him of your cooperation?"

"Of course, of course," Rashid complied quickly. "There is this girl, the dancer, and the artist who seeks Karminian. Then there are the four Russians who also look for him."

"We will take the whole list from you," the tall one said. "As you know, those I have brought are specialists in our task."

The five killers from the Casbah would, I could see, go about their business with ruthless efficiency.

I was wondering how much Rashid actually knew. Obviously, I was on the list. So was Aggie, but he hadn't mentioned Marina. Perhaps only because he hadn't gotten around to her yet.

I was just starting to inch my way backward along the narrow beam when it decided to give up. It did so with only a sudden sharp crack as a warning. I only had time to leap forward, seize the crossbar of the lintel and hang there. The beam tore

loose at the end and crashed down with the sound
of splintering wood.

The Rifs came racing into the dark of the storage
room. Hanging on with both hands, I couldn't reach
either Hugo or Wilhelmina.

They were in a cluster just below me, looking at
the fallen beam in the cloud of dust. It would be
only seconds and they'd turn their faces up and see
the figure hanging there.

I did notice that the sixth man in western dress
was not among them. He'd taken off, apparently,
and I was sure it wasn't because he was naturally
shy.

There wasn't much choice left to me so I decided
to get the advantage of surprise, at least. I let go,
dropping straight down atop the small, robed cluster. I felt my feet take out one of them, landing hard
on his head. The fall sent me sprawling and tum-
bling onto the others and I went down in a welter of
robes and flying *djellabas*.

I rolled over and was on my feet before they'd
collected themselves, racing across the lighted room
for the door. I just reached it and was tearing
through the curtained archway when the first shot
rang out, a tremendous, crashing explosion that
could only have come from an old, heavy pistol. The
bullet slammed into the wall with a crashing thud,
but I was on the streets already.

I could hear their excited shouts as they came
after me. The small, narrow street was virtually deserted, and the end of it was quite a way down. I'd
neper make it before they had me in their sights.

I ducked into a small passageway between two of
the closed gift shops. A small side door of one didn't
look too sturdy. It wasn't, and it flew open as I

slammed into it with my shoulder. I closed it behind me and moved into the darkness of the small shop.

I could make out brass kettles, a stack of small carpets, leather-covered camel saddles, water-pipes and teapots, kettles, incense burners, pottery and brass trays.

The place was a virtual booby trap. The wrong move was certain to send something crashing. I crept into a corner and rested on one knee. I could hear them outside, the tall one's voice giving instructions.

I knew enough Berber to catch the most of it. They were going to make a house-to-house search, apparently convinced I hadn't had time to make it to the end of the long street.

I stayed quietly and waited. It wasn't a long time before I heard the side door being pushed open. I watched the robed figure move cautiously into the room, the long, curved dagger unsheathed, held in one hand. Any noise, from either of us, would be heard by the others prowling outside. I watched him moving carefully into the little shop, skirting the pottery.

Hugo dropped into the palm of my hand noiselessly, the cold steel blade a comforting touch. I saw a glint that told me the Rif had his long, curved Moorish dagger unsheathed and ready. I drew back my arm and waited. This had to be right. I couldn't have him falling and crashing into copper trays or knocking over pottery.

I waited until he was slowly moving alongside the thick pile of carpets in the center of the shop. Hugo flashed through the dark, death on wings of tempered steel. I saw the Rif clutch at his chest, stagger backward and topple over onto the soft stack of carpets, noiselessly. I was beside him in an instant but there would be no final cry from him.

Quickly, I pulled off his *djellaba* and burnoose. Slipping into them, I retrieved Hugo and went out the door. I ducked out the little passageway, straightened up, and started down the street, head lowered, another Arab in his *djellaba.*

I passed two of the Rifs as they emerged from one of the shops.

They shot me a quick glance and hurried on to the next shop.

I stayed in the *djellaba* until I was out of the *medina* and then came out from under it and headed for Aggie Foster's apartment. She would be getting back from the club soon enough, and I waited outside, in the shadows of the arched doorway of the house.

Finally, I saw her approaching, hurrying toward the building. I stepped from the shadows and called to her. She jumped in fright.

"That's not funny," she said angrily.

"I wasn't trying to be funny," I said. "Come on, let's get inside."

She caught the urgency in my voice and quickly opened the door to her flat.

"Did you find Anton?" she asked, shedding her coat. She had her costume on underneath it.

"Not exactly," I answered.

I had decided to say nothing about Karminian being dead. Rashid swore he'd killed Karminian, but his fellow Rifs didn't seem to be at all certain of it. I wasn't sure I was, either.

Nothing would be helped by mentioning it to Aggie but when I told her I wanted her to clear out of town she put up such a fuss that I had to open up a little with her.

"Look, honey," I said. "Your friend Karminian was mixed up in some pretty nasty stuff, I learned. Anyone who knew him is in real danger and that definitely includes you."

She looked at me skeptically and I opened up more.

"He wasn't exactly everything you thought," I said. "He was a completely different person to some people. He seemed to have two distinct personalities. I'd say he was a real weirdo."

I tossed out a few of the smaller contradictions I'd found out without getting trapped in any details.

"So what?" Aggie answered defensively. "So he had a split personality. Back in Akron they used to say the same thing about my sister and me. We were completely different in everything, in our likes, our tastes, our habits, clothes, amusements, everything. People used to wonder how two sisters could be so different in every respect."

It had been an innocent statement and I automatically started to answer it.

"All right, but that was you and your sister," I said. "That's still two people and . . ." I left the sentence hanging in mid-air as bright lights began to explode over my head.

My thoughts burst out in a geyser of rushing, interconnected sequences. Aggie and her sister . . . two people . . . very different. What if Karminian had been two people? Brothers, identical twins?

I sat down on the arm of a stuffed chair as the enormous simplicity of it swept over me. Of course, that was it!

The out-of-focus picture was suddenly pulled into

sharp clarity, and all the contradictions and questions started to answer themselves. Two people—twins, with completely opposite personalities. It was uncommon but not unheard of. Marina and Aggie had actually known two different Karminians.

I took it a step further. What if they'd been working both sides of the street, and doing it for years, one contacting AXE with information to sell, the other contacting the Russians? They'd pool their bids and sell to the highest bidder, of course. Or, they'd supply each side with information on the other's activities.

Naturally, when our Karminian contacted Hawk, his brother had contacted the Russians. That explained what the Kremlin gremlins were doing here. Like Hawk, they too wondered what had happened to their contact when they didn't hear any further. But the importance of what I'd discovered was still incomplete.

What was the "something big" the Karminians had uncovered? And how did it concern the Rifs? They had killed one Karminian, the only one they knew existed, which meant the other one was in hiding someplace, in fear of his life.

I smiled to myself. Right now I was the only one who knew that there was a second Karminian, and that he was hiding someplace, holed up in fearful desperation. He, of course, knew the Rifs were after him, knew they'd gotten to his twin brother.

I had to find him and find him first. He was the key to everything and I wondered which one he was, the introvert or the extrovert, Marina's Karminian or Aggie's.

I watched Aggie emerge from the bedroom where she'd changed from her costume into a bathrobe.

A frightened, fearful man would undoubtedly try to contact someone for help sooner or later. By rights, I knew I ought to urge her to stick around on the chance that her Karminian was still alive. But I couldn't. It would be murder. The killers from the Casbah were on the loose, ruthlessly determined men.

I'd find Karminian some other way. Maybe they'd find him for me.

I took Aggie by the shoulders.

"You get your clothes on and take off for the airport or the bus terminal," I said. "You can contact me at the American embassy here from wherever you go if you like. But clear out, understand? Forget the Club Bedouin. The world's full of them and you'd be a smash now back in Akron. Just get going, Aggie."

She didn't say anything, her lips pushed out in a pout.

I grinned down at her. "Do as I say, honey," I asked her. "Believe me, you'll find your way someplace else. I know you're not ready, but that's not important now. Move out, sweetie. It's time."

I kissed her quickly and left, hoping I'd scared her enough to get moving.

I headed for Karminian's flat to pick up my things and find someplace else from which to operate. I was on that list Rashid had rattled off to the Casbah killers and staying in Karminian's flat like a sitting duck would only be making their task easier. They were a completely unexpected development.

I could see the Russians wanting Karminian if they suspected him of selling to us or if they knew he had hold of something big involving them. But the fierce fighters from the mountainous Rif? It just didn't fit in and yet they were in, in for murder.

I hurried through the silent, dark streets of Casablanca with the feeling that my discovery about Karminian was not the only strange twist in store for me in this thing.

# CHAPTER 4

Returning to Karminian's place for my things wasn't a poor move. It had to be done—I'd left too many things behind. It had been a long day, and I was starting to feel a little tired when I put two tubes of paint in my pocket, closed up the paint box, took a last look around the flat and then closed the door behind me.

I had just walked out the arched doorway when the two shapes appeared, one on each side of me, and I felt the hard end of two guns pressed into me. I looked at the small, hard-blue eyes of the crew-cut Russian, his lips grim, set in a thin line.

"We will kill you here if we have to," he muttered.

I saw the black Mercedes 600 pull around from the side street.

"You don't have to," I shrugged. "I'm easy to get along with."

Pig-eyes gave me a fast frisking and took Wilhelmina. Crew-cut took the paint box and handed it to the other one. They didn't have to tell me to get into the Mercedes.

I followed Crew-cut in and sat down between the

two of them. The chauffeur turned and stared at me for a moment, his eyes very much the same hard, cold blue as Crew-cut's unblinking orbs. He put the car into gear and we rolled quietly away. Two revolvers were poking into me.

It wasn't a spot for anything more than conversation.

"What's this all about?" I asked for openers.

Silence was my only answer, cold, angry silence.

"Don't tell me," I tried again. "Let me guess. Let's see now . . . you want your portrait painted."

Crew-cut glared at me but said nothing.

I tried another tack. "If you think I know where Karminian is you're wasting your time," I said.

"Neither did Ivan but it didn't stop you from killing him," Crew-cut finally answered, his voice a low snarl.

"I didn't kill anybody," I protested.

I saw the Russian lift his arm and bring it around in a short, chopping blow, the gun still gripped in his hand. It landed on my cheek and upper lip and I felt the trickle of blood that immediately ran down the side of my mouth.

"Lying pig!" he spit out. "You thought Ivan knew where Karminian was and you killed him when he refused to tell you. Now we will do the same thing to you."

My mind was racing and I deduced what had happened instantly. The Rifs had struck again but telling Crew-cut and his pals wouldn't help any.

First, I didn't want to clue them in on anything and secondly they'd never believe me anyway. All I could do for now was hold to my story.

"When was I supposed to have killed your Ivan?" I asked.

"You know very well when, swine," he barked. "When you found he was alone in the house, waiting for a radio message from Moscow."

"Why me?" I cut in. "It could have been anybody, even a thief."

"Bah!" the Russian grunted. "You seek Karminian too. It took someone with strength, someone who knew how to use the Moorish dagger. That rules out either of the women. And you are not an artist. We believe you are an American agent."

I almost said congratulations. They'd gotten one thing right anyway. But I could see where I'd be their logical suspect and I decided on a little fishing of my own.

"Did I only kill one of your men?" I asked. "There were five of you including that ape dressed up like a chauffeur."

The "ape" turned to give me a hard look.

"*Da,*" Crew-cut answered. "Panusky is at the house, waiting for us. That will leaves four of us, more than enough to take care of you."

It was a good supposition for him anyway, and I'd found out what I'd wanted to learn. There were no others I hadn't seen during our first go-round.

The Mercedes halted, and I saw the low-hanging crossbars forming part of the entranceway roof once again. I got out, and both their guns stayed in my ribs and this time the chauffeur came up behind us. They weren't taking any chances with me.

"Panusky," Crew-cut called out. "It's Estan."

There was no answer, and I felt a chilling premonition race through my body.

The Russian called out again and once more the house was silent.

I saw him frown.

"That's strange," he growled.

Pushing me along before them, they went into the inner room.

I wasn't nearly as surprised as they were.

Panusky lay on the floor in a pool of blood, his head nearly severed from his neck.

I saw the slice in his neck was a curved arc, extending from almost the back of the neck to a point just under the chin. From the freshness of the still widening pool of blood, it hadn't happened more than about fifteen minutes ago.

The Russians were staring at the man's lifeless form as if they couldn't believe their eyes.

I was thinking about the Rifs. They'd obviously been watching the place, saw the others leave and struck. They wanted to take the Russians one by one, apparently, silently, without any noisy shoot-outs.

"When did I kill him?" I asked. "When you were holding me prisoner in the car? He hasn't been dead more than fifteen or twenty minutes. Now maybe you'll believe me."

The one called Estan spoke to the others in short, rapid sentences, naturally unaware that my Russian was more than passable.

They were shaken up, alarmed, confused. Who, when and why flew in all directions but they kept their damned guns in my ribs.

Finally, Crew-cut turned to me again.

"You are not working alone," he announced. "You have others with you who did this."

"Yeah," I said. "With the Moorish dagger again. We always use them. You know, when in Rome do as the Romans do."

His hard, pig-like blue eyes studied me, and I

CK—6

could see him trying to think this out in a hurry. It took effort.

"Maybe you didn't do it," he said finally. "You might even be an artist. It really doesn't matter any longer. We will have to kill you anyway. You know too much to let you run around loose."

"I forget quickly," I said but the Russian just continued to stare at me.

Hugo was silently waiting against my forearm. It was beginning to look as though I would have to finish what the Rifs had started, if I could finish it, that is.

They kept their guns steady. One sudden move and two slugs would be meeting inside me someplace.

"Where, Estan?" the second Russian asked.

"Here," Crew-cut replied. "We'll leave his body here with Panusky's and work out of someplace else. Take Panusky's passport and identification card first. I don't like sloppy work."

The chauffeur retrieved the dead man's identity papers and I knew I had to buy some time and buy it fast.

"Wait," I said. "What if I could take you to where Karminian is staying?"

The Russian's little eyes opened wider and a slow smile of satisfaction crept over his face.

I let myself look hopeful and apprehensive.

"Well, well," he said, taking my shirt front with a ham-handed grasp. "Suddenly your memory is returning, eh?"

He shook me back and forth, and I let myself go limp.

"Where is he, pig?" he thundered.

I shook my head. "Only if you promise to let me go afterward," I said.

The Russian slowly unclenched his big hand and smiled slowly, obviously at my naïveté.

"All right," he said smoothly. "All right. We don't want to kill you. All we want is a little cooperation."

Little naïve me smiled in gratitude at his generosity. "I can't tell you where he is, but I can take you there," I said. "I only found out tonight. The place was pointed out to me by someone who saw him there."

Crew-cut did all but lick his chops. "Move," he commanded. "There's no time to waste."

Inside the Mercedes limousine again, they settled back on either side of me, guns still out and ready. The chauffeur, my paint box still on the seat beside him, moved the big car from the curb and I began to direct him up and down streets and avenues.

I put on a good act of searching for the place, looking for landmarks to help me. Actually, I was desperately looking for a spot that would give me a chance. I could feel their impatience growing as I kept the car going up and down side streets, around corners and across boulevards.

I knew I couldn't keep the charade up much longer and then, suddenly, I found it, a dark street running alongside one of the old *bidonvilles*, the tar-paper and tin-can slums that once infested the city.

During World War II, Casablanca had been a thriving port, and, at the war's end, hundreds of thousands of Arab migrants had descended on the port, lured by the promise of easy work. They set up unsightly, unsanitary slum areas that soon virtually overran the city. First the French and then the Moroccan governments attacked the problem and cleaned up many of the bidonvilles.

A number still existed, however, houses made of sheets of tin and tar-paper, nothing more than four walls and a roof, without facilities of any kind. The one I'd found was typical of its kind, its streets mere narrow passageways between the ramshackle huts.

"Stop!" I cried out.

I moved quickly and had the door open before the car came to a halt. The two Russians followed on my heels as I started into the *bidonville*. I caught a glimpse of the third one coming around the hood of the Mercedes, still keeping his chauffeur's uniform smartly buttoned up.

I moved down one of the passageways, past houses that leaned in four directions at once. Suddenly I halted outside one shack, the door ajar, and I was sure untenanted. The interior was pitch black.

"In there," I whispered to the Russian.

He motioned to the chauffeur to go around to the other side of the shack.

"Watch him," he told the other Russian, gesturing to me as he carefully started to enter the shack, pressing his back tight against the rickety, tin sheet of a door.

As Crew-cut started to move slowly into the blackness of the shack I glanced at the other Russian. He had the gun on me but his glance kept darting to the shack. It wasn't great but it was the best I could do under the circumstances.

I moved my forearm, slowly turning it as I tightened the muscles. I felt the stiletto release and drop silently into the palm of my hand. My legs tensed, coiled springs of muscle and sinew.

I watched the Russian. His eyes flicked over to

the shack. It was but a moment, but the moment was all I needed.

I threw Hugo underhanded, with all my strength, diving to the right at the same instant. The stiletto went into his belly and I heard him suck his breath in sharply.

As I'd figured, his finger automatically squeezed down on the trigger, and he got off one shot before he collapsed. Only I wasn't there. I was racing down one of the black, narrow passages that stank of urine and rotted food and of everything else.

Crew-cut would be out and after me now, as would the one masquerading as a chauffeur.

I heard their harsh shouts as they split up to take different passageways. They were making things easier for me. But I heard other sounds as the slum-dwellers began to wake. I reached a spot where two passageways bisected.

I could hear Crew-cut's footsteps racing after me and I looked around desperately for something to use as a weapon. A piece of tin, half-peeled from one of the shacks, caught my eye. It was thin but stiff, its edges jagged as a hundred slivers of broken glass.

I grabbed at it and pulled it free, feeling the blood spurt from my hands where they dug into the jagged edge. The small sheet of tin in my hands, I dropped to one knee in the deepest shadows against the shack.

Crew-cut emerged from the passageway and halted, peering up and then down the bisecting passage.

The mind is a funny thing, and suddenly I was seeing a little boy a long time ago standing on the shore of a lake and skipping flat stones far out across the water. It was the same motion, a short, hard flick of the wrist. I took aim and let the sheet of tin fly.

Crew-cut turned just as it slammed into his face, the jagged edge a hundred bits of tearing, ripping metal. Blood leaped from his face. He screamed in pain, dropped the gun and threw both hands up to his face.

I dived for the gun, grabbed it and pressed it against his stomach. I fired twice, the shots partially muffled in his clothes.

Now there was only one Russian left and I moved back into the shadows of the shack. I had only moments to wait.

He came racing down, saw the inert form of Crew-cut sprawled in the intersection and whirled, blazing away at every corner. He was firing wildly but furiously, and the slugs were zinging into the tin all around me.

I dropped to a prone position and fired back.

He staggered as my shots tore into him, but he stayed on his feet, still firing back, and now he had a bead on me.

I felt one slug tear through my collar, and I rolled over to come up against the shack.

Steadying my arm against the tin wall, I risked the time to aim, and my shot caught him right between the eyes.

He did a backflip and lay still.

I walked over to him and his uniformed chauffeur's coat had ripped open to reveal the reason for his durability. He was wearing a steel, bullet-proof vest, the kind the European cops wear for riot duty.

I looked at the gun in my hand, tried the chamber and saw it was empty. The torrent of shots had set the neighborhood to waking, and lights and shouts filled the air.

I ran, tossing the useless gun away, as dawn lightened the sky, and I heard the sudden, sharp wail of a police siren nearby.

I wanted to retrieve Hugo but there wasn't time to go back, not with the Casablanca cops just around the corner. I found my way through the *bidonville* and back to the Mercedes where, I saw happily, the keys were still in the ignition.

As I slid behind the wheel and drove off unhurriedly, I passed two police cruisers, lights flashing and sirens wailing beneath the fast-rising day.

I headed for Marina, but Aggie's place was on the way, and I turned off to pull to a halt across the street from her apartment. If she hadn't left yet I'd drive her to the airport myself.

I bounded up the steps and saw the door to her apartment ajar, the sight a sudden mixture of hope and fear, hope that it meant she'd cleared out fast, fear that it meant she hadn't been fast enough.

I pushed the door open slowly. It was the fear that won out.

Aggie Foster would never see Akron, Ohio, again. She lay on the floor, half-dressed, her throat nearly slashed in two and, as it had been with the Russian, with the same, curving arc.

I knelt down beside her and gently moved her legs. There was no evidence that she'd been touched otherwise. It was a killing, silently, efficiently and an icy rage churned inside me. The sneaking, murdering bastards would pay for this.

I had already reduced their number from five to four, not counting Rashid. I'd reduce it to zero.

The cold rage inside me welled up, but I fought it

down. This was no time for wild rages. This called for the same silent, deadly efficiency they practiced. But now another fear swept over me, and I raced out of the building and into the Mercedes, roaring from the curb in a screech of complaining rubber.

Glad for the still empty streets of the early morning, I tooled the big car along the Avenue de l'Hippodrome, took the corner into the Boulevard Zerktouni on two wheels and came to a tire-marked spot across the street from Marina's apartment on Hassan Souktany. My eyes swept the area as I dashed into the building. Only a beggar wandered down the street.

I pounded on the door and allowed a sigh of relief to escape me as I heard the lock click open from inside.

Marina opened the door a slit, her eyes half-closed yet, and then they opened wider as she saw me.

I pushed my way in and frowned, glancing quickly about.

She was in a half-slip and a bra, her shoes beside the small hassock in front of the sofa.

The bedroom door was open and I saw the bed fully made.

She'd been sleeping on the sofa in her slip and bra. She avoided my inquiring glance.

"Insomnia?" I asked quietly.

"As a matter of fact, yes," she said quickly, rubbing her hands across her face. "I . . . I was reading, and I must have fallen asleep on the sofa."

"You must have put the book away first," I said, glancing around.

"Why, yes . . . I guess I did," she stammered nervously. She picked her dress up from the end of the sofa and put it on a hanger.

I watched the beautiful movement of her breasts as she stretched her arms up to hang the dress.

"You don't seem exactly elated at seeing me," I tossed out.

She turned and a small furrow darkened her brow.

"It . . . it's not that." she said. "It's just that I . . . I'm not feeling very well this morning. I . . . I'm going to try to sleep some more. I'll call you later."

I was seeing the gorgeous raven-haired creature who wouldn't let me go till I promised to return. Something was very wrong here. I could see it in her quick, almost furtive glances, the nervous little flutter of her hands.

"No, you're not going to call me later," I said. "You're going to leave here at once."

Her eyes grew wide. "Leave here?" she gasped. "Why, that's impossible. I . . . I can't. It . . . it's ridiculous."

"Not as ridiculous as getting killed," I said.

Marina swallowed hard. "Getting killed?" she repeated.

"You friend Karminian was mixed up in some nasty business," I said. "Because you knew him you're in great danger. A number of people have been killed already."

As I spoke I heard myself sounding like a playback, an echo of a previous speech.

"All right," she said, quickly. "I'll leave . . . tomorrow. I've got to stay here today."

She was trying to placate me.

"Why must you stay here today?" I asked, watching her closely.

Her lips tightened and she turned away for a moment. When she turned back she had composed herself.

"Someone is coming here," she said. "An old aunt of mine. I've got to stay here and wait for her. It concerns important family matters, trouble at home."

"Okay," I said. "Then I'll stay too. I think you need protecting." I smiled grimly, inwardly.

Her story was as phony as a three dollar bill.

The alarm in her eyes when I announced I was staying was final proof, not that I needed it.

"No, Glen . . . you can't stay," she said, coming over to me. "It . . . it's very confidential. Please, understand."

I smiled. I was understanding a lot of things, mostly that she didn't want me around.

Her face was now strained and white. Whatever was bothering her had brought her to a steel wire tenseness.

I noted, too, that she hadn't seemed at all surprised when I mentioned that Karminian had been mixed up in some pretty nasty business. Maybe she knew it already. Maybe she was mixed up in it too. It was a possibility I couldn't discard.

I had a suspicion that was taking larger shape with every passing second. This lovely creature, so frantically hungering so recently, was desperately trying to get rid of me. She was hiding something.

Five men and one girl had already been killed and I had a job to do. The time for playing games was over.

I watched her as she came over to me, the rapid rise and fall of her breasts exciting and tempting. But she could have been the Goddess of Love now, and it wouldn't have bothered me.

I was on the trail of something and that's all that counted.

"Please, Glen," she said. "Do it my way and I'll explain tonight."

I smiled and sat down. "You won't be able to explain anything to anyone tonight if I leave you alone," I said. "I don't mind sitting around, really. I'll go into the other room when your aunt gets here so you can talk privately."

Marina whirled around, angry frustration mirrored in her face.

I picked up a magazine and casually started to thumb through it.

Marina paced back and forth a few times, went into the kitchen, came out again and sat down, got up again, walked to the window and sat down again.

"Something bothering you, doll?" I asked casually.

"Yes," she snapped. "This whole thing. It's just silly. It just won't work this way. I want you to leave and I'll call you after my aunt's gone."

I got up slowly, smiling, and she didn't read the cold deadliness in it. "All right, sweetie," I said. "After I do one thing."

"What's that?" she asked quickly.

I walked over to where she sat, looked down at her and then shot out a hand and grabbed the black bra in the center. As I yanked her up and onto her feet, the bra pulled down and her lovely breasts sprang free.

"After I get the truth out of you," I snarled.

She tried to tear free, but I had her wrist now, and I whirled her around and slammed her down on the rug.

Her eyes were wide with helpless fear.

"The truth, Marina, and quick," I said.

"You . . . you're hurting me," she said.

I loosened my grip on her wrist and with my other hand, began to caress the soft, smooth pink tips of her breasts.

"Sorry," I said. "Is this better?"

Her eyes, black with anger at first, began to change to something else.

"Stop it," she cried. "Stop it."

I felt the smooth tips begin to grow hard and rise at my caresses. I continued to stroke them, gently, rhythmically.

"Oh, God, please stop," she gasped out. "Please, Glen . . . don't."

"When did you hear from him?" I asked suddenly, taking my hand from her breast at the same time.

She looked up at me, her lower lip quivering.

I touched her nipple again and freed her other arm. "The truth, Marina," I said softly. "Tell me."

Her eyes looked up at me, suddenly filled with tears, and then she broke, flinging her face against my chest and sobbing, short, gasping sobs.

I held her tight.

"Where is he?" I asked firmly. "Come on, Marina. Tell me."

"I don't know," she sobbed into my chest. "He called last night. I promised I wouldn't tell anyone."

"I want to help you," I said. "And him too."

She pulled her head back and wiped the tears from her eyes.

I let her sit up.

"He's going to call me again this morning, sometime, when he can get to a phone," she blurted out. "He has money in a locker and the key someplace. I'm to get the key, take the money and bring it to him. He'll give me full instructions when he calls back."

"That's why you dozed on the sofa," I finished for her. "You wanted to be ready the moment he called."

She nodded. She was telling the truth, all she knew, and this was my golden opportunity to find Karminian.

I needed her cooperation. I didn't want her trying to give me the slip when she went to meet him so I decided to level with her, telling her as much as I knew.

I began with the two Karminians and their activities as espionage informants and when I'd finished she was pale and shaken, her eyes deep and round.

"I would never have believed it," she said quietly. "And you aren't an artist at all, then. I was right in suspecting that, Glen."

"Oh, I've been called an artist in my work." I grinned. "And you can stop calling me Glen. It's Nick—Nick Carter."

"Nick," she said, turning it over in her mind, savoring it aloud. "Yes, it fits you better," she said finally. "It fits that sense of urgency and danger I first felt about you."

Marina leaned forward and I had to hold back from scooping those two beautiful breasts up in my hands.

"Poor Anton," she said sadly.

"Which Karminian has contacted you?" I asked. "Did you hear any voice difference?"

"Why, it had to be my Anton," she replied. "I doubt the other one knew I existed, and only my Anton knew the little things between us he mentioned. Promise me he won't be hurt, Nick. I feel terrible enough about going back on my word to him."

"My people won't hurt him," I answered. "The Russians have other methods but they're out of the picture now. The Rifs will certainly kill him. They might torture him to find out exactly how much he knows, first. And you shouldn't feel horrible about having told me. You're doing him a hell of a favor. You're saving his neck."

She put her head against my shoulder. It would have been so easy to take her in my arms and make love to her but I didn't. That was not something I wanted to have stopped in the middle by a phone call. Not with Marina.

As it was, we didn't have to wait long. When the phone jangled, Marina's eyes flew to mine and her lips tightened.

"Answer it," I said firmly. "Be yourself. Loosen up."

She swallowed hard, picked up the phone and I watched her as she spoke to him, her eyes riveted on me all the while.

"Yes, yes, Anton," she said. "I'm ready. Yes . . . I know the place. In your name. I understand. All right. I'll be there with it. Yes, Anton. *Au 'voir.*"

She put down the phone and I was beside her at once.

"Let's go," I said, pulling her to her feet.

She slipped on her dress and I rushed her out the door.

"What's the plan?" I said brusquely. "Let's have it."

"The key to the locker is at the Hotel Mahraba in an envelope in his name," she said. "He told the desk clerk I would be picking it up. The locker is at the Main Post Office at the Place des Nations Unies."

"So far so good," I commented as we got into the Mercedes. "After you get the money where do you go?"

She looked at me, hesitated a moment, and then answered. "To the Marcel Cerdan Stadium. It is not in use today, and I'm to go to section fourteen, aisle B and wait there."

The Marcel Cerdan Stadium, I repeated to myself. I'd passed it once. It was modern, huge, typical of its kind, named after the French middleweight champion killed in an air crash some years ago. I wondered grimly if he'd been hiding in the stadium all along. He could mingle with the crowds when it was in use and hide away when it closed.

It was vast enough to avoid the cleaning brigades and the night watchman. He could probably pilfer food from concession stands too. An ingenious spot to pick, but then I'd already learned the Karminian twins had a long record of ingenious schemes.

"After you get the money from the locker, you'll take a taxi to the stadium," I told Marina. "Go through with everything just as you've been instructed by him."

I wondered about reaching the stadium unseen. Such places usually had large, wide-open spaces around them. That was a problem I'd have to meet when I got there. I shot Marina another glance and saw her watching me apprehensively.

"What's the matter?" I asked sharply.

"I . . . I don't know if I've done the right thing," she answered. "Suddenly you frighten me. You're so different, so predatory, like a leopard that's suddenly scented a kill."

She shuddered and I didn't try to smooth it over.

"Occupational conditioning," I said. "It's too late to change your mind now, Marina."

I glanced at her again and saw she was still looking apprehensive and unhappy. I decided that the unhappy facts of life might straighten her out, just in case she got any last minute ideas.

"I'm going to be there, Marina," I said. "If you go through with things, I'll be able to grab him and get him to safety. But I can't let him get away. If you try to help him escape I'll shoot him."

I omitted the fact that I didn't have a gun with me.

"You would, wouldn't you?" she said, shock lacing her words.

"You can count on it, baby," I said. I braked to a halt outside the Mahraba Hotel. "Get the key," I ordered. "And let's keep moving."

She got out, giving me a hurt, shocked look but I knew she'd play it straight now. In minutes she was back with an envelope which she opened as I wheeled the car toward the complex of buildings known as United Nations Plaza.

Once again I drew up and waited outside as she hurried into the building. This time she reappeared carrying a small satchel, not unlike an airlines bag. She unzipped it in the car and I didn't bother to count the neatly wrapped packages of bills. There was a lot of money in the bag, perhaps ten or fifteen thousand dollars, I guessed. She zipped the bag up again and I pulled to the curb behind a taxi stand.

"Take one of those cabs and follow through with the plan," I said. "Don't look for me, don't think about me. I'll show up at the right time."

I watched as she walked to the nearest of the taxis

and climbed in, the long, lovely line of her leg disappearing into the rear of the old cab.

She hadn't said a thing, and I could feel the nervous tension in her but I was confident she'd stick with it.

I followed the cab for a while, and, as we neared the stadium, I swung down a side street and gunned the limousine in a roaring race to the stadium. I pulled over a block from it and went the rest of the way on foot.

As I'd feared, the area around the place was open space.

Karminian would no doubt be watching, perhaps from high up in the seats, with a falcon's view covering every part of the outside of the oval. He'd be certain to see me approaching.

A sound behind me made me whirl and I saw a man with a small cart of fruits coming down the street, a gaily colored parasol covering his little two-wheeled cart.

I waited till he passed abreast of me, then quickly moved behind him. I applied just enough pressure, carefully, slowly, and he sank to the ground unconscious.

It was risky business. The least little bit too much and he'd be dead. I put him against the building after I checked his heart. He was breathing normally, and he'd wake within five minutes.

I took the cart and started pushing it out into the open space surrounding the stadium. Beneath the bright parasol, I was only a pair of legs, slowly pushing a little fruit cart.

I passed the door marked *Cinq* and went on close to the concrete stadium wall. I was beyond the line of vision of anyone watching from inside. I passed another door and paused to push against it. It was locked and steel ribbed. I went on past two more locked doors until I came to a small, narrow doorway. This one was wood and I halted the little cart to push against it. It was locked but the wood yielded.

I turned to see the taxi draw up back beside the first of the doors and Marina get out.

Karminian would be watching her now. I stepped back, hit the door with my shoulder, timing it to coincide with the noise of the taxi engine starting up, and half-fell, half-stumbled into the dimness of the interior of the stadium.

I was beneath the seats and I moved along the passageways, working my way back toward the main entrance to the stadium. I could hear the sharp sound of Marina's heels clicking along the concrete flooring up ahead and I saw the arrow directing spectators to Row B. I followed it, moving slowly now.

As I passed Row A I cut up and out onto the seating area. Almost creeping, crouched low behind the rows of seats, I peered over at Marina's figure as she stood alone, waiting in aisle B.

I gazed across the thousands of empty seats, looking for a figure, but there was only silence. I stayed crouched behind the seats, peering out through a small opening between two of them.

He had been terribly clever, cautious and fearful up to now, and he would continue to be.

I could see Marina, now beginning to pace up and down, her eyes scanning the empty stadium. He might be anywhere, waiting, watching.

Then, suddenly, I saw him, a small black shape half-way across the stadium, making his way along the passageway where the seats sloped down to the edge of the field.

Marina hadn't seen him yet, and he was still pacing nervously. It was only when he drew near that she saw him and whirled to wave at him.

I saw her glance around quickly, and I knew she was trying to spot me.

Knock it off, I hissed inwardly. You'll get him suspicious.

She waved to him again, and now he was mounting the steps from the lower seats, taking them in bounds.

He was fairly tall, black-haired, with the gaunt, cadaverous kind of good looks that make women feel protective.

Marina rushed over to him and I noted that he took the bag first and then embraced her.

"Anton," I heard Marina say. "I've done what was best for you."

I saw him frown at once. She'd have him on guard and running with talk like that. It was time to move and move fast. I didn't know how true that was as I leaped over the seats and headed for them.

He whirled and saw me at once. He turned to Marina and his arm shot out. I saw her recoil as the slap struck her face and echoed like a small shot in the emptiness of the stadium.

"Bitch!" he shouted at her.

"No, Anton, no!" Marina cried but he was off and running.

I was moving through a row of seats to cut him off when we suddenly had company. I saw the evil face of Rashid first as he appeared at the top of the sloping ramp between the rows of seats. Then I saw the other four, moving in from all sides. My first thought was to wonder how the hell they knew we were there, but I tossed aside speculation for action.

Karminian saw them also, and I caught a glimpse of Marina's shocked face.

I was closest to him, and I reached out and grabbed his arm.

"Stay with me," I hissed at him.

He paused a second, and I thought he was going to go along. Instead, he turned and kicked out, his ascetic face livid with rage. The blow took me by surprise and I felt the sharp, stabbing pain in the groin. I went down on one knee.

"Come back, you damn fool," I yelled at him. "I want to help you."

He wasn't listening. He was running, leaping over seats, twisting back and forth, racing up and down aisles.

One of the Rifs was coming across to cut him off, the jeweled, curved, Moorish dagger in his hand.

I couldn't let Karminian be killed. He was my only key to this. If he got away I'd find him again, somehow. Dead, there'd only be the Rifs left, and they, I knew, would fade away like a desert mirage.

Another Rif, the tall one, was coming up behind to box Karminian into a corner where two aisles bisected.

I went after Karminian as he started to leap over seats and I forced him to turn and head back toward the Rif with the unsheathed dagger. As he neared the Rif, I vaulted over a row of seats and put myself between the Arab and Karminian.

Seizing the moment, the fleeing informant cut off to the other side and streaked up the aisle.

Snarling, the Rif brought his dagger around in a sharp arc at me. As it curved through the air, I dropped level with the top of the seats and saw it come down to slice through the wooden seats in a shower of splinters.

I popped up, grabbed the Rif's arm before he could draw it back again and yanked him forward. As he toppled over the back of the seats I chopped him with a karate blow that came up to shatter his Adam's apple. He gurgled once and collapsed at my feet.

I made a grab for the dagger as it fell from his hands. I missed and it slipped under the seats. This was no time to try to find it.

The other Rif, the tall one, was only a few feet from me and I saw him hesitate, wondering who to go after.

I made up his mind for him by moving toward him.

He turned on me, drawing his own dagger.

Beyond him, I saw Karminian's form catapulting seats and racing down aisles, eluding the other Rifs.

I jumped two seats into one of the aisles and raced for the exit when I heard Marina scream. I'd lost sight of her and expected she had fled in the confusion and the melee, but now I saw Rashid throw her to the ground.

I shifted direction and went for him. He turned from Marina to me.

The tall Rif was coming up behind me, dagger in hand.

The other two, I saw, were zeroing in from the sides.

I halted, half-crouched, feeling like a deer cornered by a pack of wolves.

Rashid drew his dagger and started for me, but the tall Rif called out, and he halted.

"No, do not kill him," he commanded. "I want him and the girl alive."

I breathed an inaudible sigh of relief, straightened up and let my muscles relax.

The other two Rifs were pulling Marina to her feet now, and I saw her face, white, terror-stricken, strained.

I felt the point of the dagger in the small of my back, and I was surrounded in seconds.

The tall one holding the dagger against me only gave me a passing glance and I saw his eyes were riveted on Rashid.

"So, Rashid, son of a mud-caked pig," he snarled. "You killed Karminian, did you?"

I watched Rashid's eyebrows go up in protest. "But I did kill him, I tell you," the Rif answered excitedly.

"You not only lie, you persist in maintaining the charade," the tall one shouted. "Your lying tongue will not wag again."

He motioned to the other two Rifs who started for Rashid, daggers drawn.

Rashid's evil face had broken into a mask of abject terror. He backed up, flung down his dagger and fell on his knees.

"I beg you to believe me," he croaked.

"I believe my eyes," the tall Rif spat out, nodding again to the othed two.

Rashid got up and turned to flee with a long moan of terror. The other two took after him, and I saw Marina's wide, round eyes looking at me, a frown of incredulity on her face.

My eyes, narrowed, returning her gaze, told her to keep her mouth shut. I knew damn well what she was thinking, that I knew the explanation, that I could prevent this miscarriage of justice.

Not me, sister, I said inwardly. It's nothing more than his past evils catching up with the bastard.

I heard Rashid scream, a high-pitched scream cut off by a bone-chilling gurgling sound followed by a sickening half-scream, half-groan.

The two Rifs returned and tossed something on the concrete in front of the tall one.

I looked at the bloody, grisly object for a moment before realizing it was Rashid's tongue.

I looked up at Marina, saw her eyes roll upward as she fell into a dead faint. I caught her before she hit the ground.

"We will take these two back to El Ahmid," the tall one said. "He will find ways to make them tell us where Karminian hides."

"We don't know anything about that," I said. "Neither I nor the girl know."

The Rif smiled, a slow, nasty smile. "That is why she came here with the money," he said, sarcasm dripping from his tone. "That is why you interfered and let him escape us."

"I had my own reasons for that," I answered, gently slapping Marina's cheeks. "How did you know we were meeting him here?" I questioned further.

Their sudden appearance still bugged me. I'd seen no signs of them or of being tailed by anyone.

The tall Rif smiled.

"We merely applied the techniques of our mountains to the city," he said. "We put a man atop the minaret on the top of the Great Mosque. He saw the streets of the city as we see the mountain passes from our lookout points high in the mountains. We saw you escape from the Russians in their big, black car. It was easy to follow your path in the car. When we saw you come to the stadium, park the car and proceed on foot, we converged here."

I smiled grimly. I'd gotten an object lesson in why they'd successively given the French, British and Spanish a hard time. Not only were their techniques good, but they knew how to adapt them to fit changing conditions, the first rule of military tactics.

"You are an American agent, of course," the Rif said. "And the girl is your accomplice. Karminian had been working for you."

"I am an artist," I said. "The girl knows nothing. She was an old girl friend of Karminian's."

I saw the Rif flick his eyes at one of the others who had moved behind me.

Holding Marina in my arms, I tried to turn but the sharp pain exploded in my head, bright lights flashing briefly and then a curtain of blackness.

# CHAPTER 5

I thought they'd turned me into a mummy. I was still alive and they'd mummified me; my thoughts leaped in alarm as consciousness slowly returned. Conscious of being shrouded in yards of fabric, I began to focus my blurred vision and slowly realized that I could see out through a small opening in the material. I tried to move my arms and felt the restricting pressure of wrist bonds.

I was in semi-darkness on the flat of my back, bouncing and jouncing in what was obviously a wagon. I managed to turn my head and saw another shape alongside me, wrapped in a kind of shroud, and I presumed I was similarly encased.

Glancing upward, I saw the wagon was entirely enclosed, and it dawned on me that they were transporting us in a funeral wagon, a wagon used to haul bodies shrouded for transport to burial pyres.

I couldn't tell if Marina was conscious or not, and I was thinking of perhaps kicking out at her to see when the bouncing suddenly came to a stop. The wagon had halted, and in a few moments I heard the sound of hinges creaking, and the bright glare of sunlight illuminated the interior of the wagon. I felt hands pulling me out of the rear of the wagon, and I murmured to let them know I was awake.

They stood me up and the shroud was ripped from me.

I saw the tall Rif, malevolently watching me, and I looked down at my bound wrists.

"Cut him loose," he ordered, and one of the others freed me with one deft slice of his curved dagger.

I saw Marina, awake and free of her shroud, also being cut loose.

We were out of Casablanca, halted at the side of a road. It was a hot, dry place, and I saw the horses tied up to the back of the funeral wagon. They had simply used the funeral wagon to get us quietly out of Casablanca. Now, I saw, they were going to transfer us to horseback.

"Suppose I can't ride," I said to the tall Rif suddenly.

"Then this will be your first, and last lesson," he growled.

I got the message.

I glanced at the horses and had to smile. They didn't miss a bet in their own, subtle ways.

There were four of the powerful, fleet Arabian stallions, one for each of the Rifs, and two short-legged, sturdy but slow mounts. To try escaping on them would be like trying to run from a Maserati with a Volkswagen. They wouldn't even have to watch us closely.

Sure of themselves, they mounted their Arabians at a short command from the tall Rif and waited as Marina and I climbed onto our horses.

"Don't look so dejected," I said to her as we started off after the Rifs. "You're still alive. We'll pull out of this."

It was a piece of reassurance I wished had more substance behind it. I spurred my horse on to gallop up to the tall Rif. He turned at my approach, unperturbed, staring confidently at me.

"Where are you taking us?" I asked. "The Casbah at Tangiers?"

"No," he said. "That is our official base only. We take you to our operational base, the Casbah built by El Ahmid atop Mount Dersa. He awaits us there."

I dropped back to ride beside Marina.

Mount Dersa, in the heart of the Rif mountains, where, during the Rif war, Abd-el-Krim commanded his forces that held the city of Tetuan at bay for months.

I was beginning to wonder if this El Ahmid fancied himself another Abd-el-Krim, a leader of another Rif rebellion. I was to find out he fancied himself a lot more than that.

The Rifs set a fast pace though I knew their Arabians were capable of much greater speeds for sustained periods.

I was perspiring heavily under the broiling sun, and I glanced at Marina to see her dress so wet it looked almost as though she'd fallen into a lake with it on.

It clung to her with revealing tightness, outlining every curve of her large breasts, the small pointed tips. It clung provocatively to the long line of her thighs and dipped in a deep V at the abdomen. Her cascade of black hair streamed out behind her and she had assumed a different kind of beauty, a wildness, an untamed abandon.

Marina was part Spanish and part Moroccan she'd told me, and the Spanish blood in her had surfaced so that she seemed to be a wild gypsy from the hills of Andalusia.

I had the flaring desire to pull her from the saddle and make love to her in her wildness, and I knew that if I felt that way, the Rifs must surely have the same thoughts.

But, I had already seen, they were not a band of surly cutthroats but a highly disciplined group. They might think it but they wouldn't do it.

Marina, her face wet and shiny, rode with a determined, almost angry abandon, and I knew she was trying to force anger to override fear. Until we halted at a *zitoun*, an olive grove, to water the horses, I thought she might have succeeded. I knew better when she stood beside me and watched the Rifs water their magnificent stallions.

"What's going to happen to us, Nick?" she said. "Why don't they just kill us and get it over with if that's what they intend doing?"

I could have told her that would be too easy. I didn't though.

She'd have time enough to learn what they had in store. I didn't know myself, but I had a pretty fair idea it wasn't a friendly fireside chat.

"They want to ask us some questions, I think," I told her. I didn't elaborate on their methods of asking.

The Rifs had finished watering the horses and gestured for us to mount up. The sun was lower in the sky and the rays less burning as we set off again.

I'd checked to make certain the two tubes of paint were still in my back pocket.

The Rifs had searched me, of course, when I was unconscious and decided the paint was harmless enough. They were my sole weapons at the moment, and they had limited uses.

I decided Marina and I were captive for a while yet, until I could find some moment for a break. I used the word "until" to myself. It was less pessimistic than "unless."

We rode on, and the hot day finally gave way to the coolness of night as we reached the foothills of the Rif mountain stronghold.

Once more the Rifs paused but only for a few moments at the shores of a *dayat*, a mountain lake. Now, in the darkness, two of them rode behind Marina and me.

We pushed on, and the terrain changed from the semi-desert flatness to mountain defiles and narrow passes.

Marina was having trouble staying awake and I watched her closely. She was strained, haggard, thoroughly exhausted.

I was feeling it myself, and I was surprised she'd held out this long. Even the motion of the horse no longer served to keep her awake. I saw her eyes close, watched as she began to fall from the saddle and was there to catch her as she toppled.

I reined to a halt and was surrounded by Rifs at once.

"She can't go on," I said, holding the girl in my arms.

The tall one spoke brusquely to the others, and Marina was pulled from my arms and flung like a sack of grain across the saddle on her stomach, her head and legs hanging from the sides.

With a few quick turns of rope they lashed her in place, handed the reins of the horse to me, and started off again at the same, hard-driving pace.

Don't the bastards ever get tired, I wondered. Suddenly the roads were steeper and the progress slower. We had reached Mount Dersa, I was certain.

We'd ridden most of the night, and I scanned the sky for the first hint of approaching dawn. It hadn't bowed in yet when suddenly, turning a sharp curve in a narrow pass, we came to the dark silhouette of a citadel, two heavy towers at each corner standing guard over a collection of intertwining, connected buildings.

It was the Casbah of El Ahmid, and though he may have built it in recent years it followed the architectural lines of the ancient traditional Casbahs or citadels.

The main entranceway, tall and arched, stood open, protected only by sentries.

We rode through it and halted inside a stone courtyard.

I saw other Rifs on the walls and on the ground platforms of the two towers.

They unstrapped Marina and she slid to the ground, waking up as she did so. She tried to get up but her cramped, aching muscles refused to respond.

Two Rifs yanked her to her feet and started to drag her away.

"In the women's quarters," the tall one side. "Tell the eunuchs to guard her."

He turned to me. "El Ahmid will see you after he awakens and breakfasts," he said. "Meanwhile, you will have a few hours to think about what will happen to you if you do not cooperate with us."

"I'll think carefully," I said. "That's a promise."

I was already thinking as they started to lead me away, only not what they wanted me to think about. I was noting that the wall from the towers was considerably higher than the roofs of the interconnected buildings at the back of the Casbah. I also noticed that the wall didn't enclose the rear part of the Casbah but only butted up against the structures.

When they led me down a flight of stone steps, I had formed a pretty good mental picture of the outside layout of the place. A barred door swung open, and I was shoved into a dank, stone cell, windowless and barren except for some straw piled in a corner.

"Remind me not to stop here again," I muttered to the two Rifs.

They looked at me blankly, slammed the door and took up positions at each side of it. They would be standing guard through the remainder of the night. It didn't matter much because I wasn't ready to move yet.

The cold, stone floor was hard but at least I could stretch out and flex my aching muscles.

I thought of what the tall one had said about cooperating with him, and I had to laugh, ruefully. I couldn't cooperate if I wanted to do so. Where Karminian might be hiding was as much a mystery to me as to them. However, I knew I'd never be able to convince them of that.

Instead, I'd try for the brass ring on my own. I'd try to find out what this was all about. They'd tabbed me for an American agent, anyway. I had nothing to lose by trying, nothing except my neck, that is, and I was used to risking that.

I fell asleep on the stone floor, still wondering how I came to be here and where these fierce, mountain tribesmen fitted into this weird puzzle of double-dealing twin informants.

I was wakened as the barred door came open with the sound of creaking hinges.

The two Rifs were inside the room and yanking me to my feet.

I could have taken them both, but it wasn't time yet. I didn't want to win a battle and lose the war.

"El Ahmid awaits you, pig," the one snarled, shoving me out of the cell.

I was led back up the stairs and into a long room which in turn entered upon a room of rich draperies, incense, thick carpets and thick cushions casually strewn about.

At the far end I saw a man, wearing a traditional Arab headdress with open-necked shirt and riding breeches. He sat upon a bed of the cushions.

Beside him, feeding him olives and grapes, perched on her knees, was a girl, slim, narrow-waisted, wearing a diaphonous skirt and a bra, her midriff bare. Her nose was long and broadened at the base, her eyes a glistening black and her hair flowing loosely down her back. She was fascinating without being beautiful, her breasts swelling up from the bra in twin mounds of olive-skinned provocativeness.

The two Rifs with me bowed low, almost prostrating themselves before the man.

His face was long and angular with a high, broad forehead and a long, thin nose over finely molded, chiseled lips. It was an imperious face, arrogant, cruel and supremely confident. His eyes, dark and piercing, regarded me with disdain.

"Bow when you come before El Ahmid, son of a sow," he hissed, his eyes boring into mine.

"I forget how," I smiled.

I saw the sneer in his eyes change to anger. I shot a casual glance at the girl.

Her eyebrows were raised in astonishment. It was

obvious that one didn't give smart answers to El Ahmid.

He caught my glance and rose to his feet. He was tall, six feet, I judged.

"Bow!" he commanded, eyes glaring, one hand pointing to the door.

I knew what I was doing and I did it deliberately. I'd throw him off balance, open him up. It wouldn't take much. He wasn't used to anything but abject obedience.

"Go to hell," I answered laconically.

He muttered an oath, reached down beneath one of the cushions and brought out a riding quirt. In two long steps he was before me, lashing out with the quirt.

I only moved my head to take the blow alongside my face. I felt the trickle of blood as the quirt bit sharply, painfully into the side of my face. I looked past him at the girl.

She was watching every move with eager interest.

He was standing with the quirt upraised, waiting for me to bow or receive another blow.

I bent my knees slightly, as though I were about to go down, and brought up a whistling right from behind my back. It cracked against his jaw like a rifle shot and he went crashing backward, sending cushions flying in all directions as he hit the floor.

The girl was at his side almost before he hit the floor, cradling his head in her lap, running her hands across his face. But her eyes were on me with a continuing astonishment, now tinged with something else, possibly respect.

The two Rifs had flung themselves at me and each one held an arm.

I didn't try to pull away and stood casually, relaxed.

El Ahmid was up on one elbow, a trickle of blood running from the corner of his mouth.

The girl wiped it away, solicitously.

He angrily shook her off and got to his feet.

"Let him go," he said to the two Rifs, who stepped back at once. "He shall die a thousand deaths for this," he added.

I watched the girl move to his side as he sat down on the cushions again. She was more than just a servant girl in the way she hovered over him, attentive to his every need. She was in his special favor, and she wanted to stay that way. In the way she patted his cut lip with a soft cloth, I wondered if perhaps she was in love with him. No matter, really. She was more than enough involved, and an idea was rapidly taking shape inside my nasty little mind.

El Ahmid pushed her away as a commotion from behind me was heard and I turned to see two more Rifs bringing in Marina.

She had been stripped down to black bra and black bikini panties, and she was one damn beautiful woman, her long legs curving gently to the V of her abdomen, her breasts, larger and fuller than the Arab girl's, thrusting out of the bra.

The Rifs pushed her forward, in front of El Ahmid.

I saw her cast an anguished glance at me as they went past, but mostly I watched El Ahmid and saw his eyes widen appreciatively.

He roamed up and down and across Marina's tall, full figure, devouring her with his eyes, and I saw that he had her mentally in bed already.

I also saw the Berber girl watching him, her eyes

narrowing. With the eternal female wisdom of her sex, she knew danger to her interests when she saw it.

The idea inside my head was gathering momentum fast.

El Ahmid had risen and walked around Marina, examining her from every side, as though he were about to purchase a thoroughbred.

Marina stood still, chin thrust out, only the rapid rise and fall of her lovely breasts revealing the anguished turmoil churning inside her.

With typical Arab arrogance, El Ahmid halted before me, and the superior disdain was in his eyes again.

"You are an American agent," he said. "We are certain of that. She is your woman?"

"That's right," I said. "Mine and mine alone."

Marina turned, and her eyes darkened as she gazed at me.

I didn't like using her this way, but I knew what El Ahmid's convoluted reasoning would do with that tidbit of information, and I was completely right.

"She is no longer yours, American," he announced. "She belongs to El Ahmid."

I laughed and saw the anger leap in his eyes.

"She will never give of herself to a mere mountain bandit leader," I said. Moving quickly, I stepped over to Marina and tore the brassiere from her breasts.

El Ahmid's eyes widened in desire as he gazed at Marina's gorgeous cream-white mounds.

"These are for a man of importance, a man of action," I said. "I know this woman. She will obey and submit only to the very best of men. You are a nothing."

He stepped forward, about to strike, but halted himself, eyes ablaze with anger. "The name El Ahmid will be known to all the world," he raged. "She will be happy to be at the side of El Ahmid."

"Why?" I asked mockingly. "Is he going to rob a big caravan?"

"El Ahmid will lead the new conquest of Europe," he shot out. "El Ahmid will make history repeat itself once again."

I'd hit paydirt and I pressed on.

"El Ahmid is as full of empty talk as an old man," I answered, quoting an old Moroccan proverb.

This time his temper exploded, and he brought the quirt down hard in repeated blows.

I flinched back under them, half-turning away to take them on my shoulder.

Two Rifs seized me and turned me around. The damned quirt cut painfully across my temple and then my jawbone, and I could feel the rivulets of blood starting to trail down along my skin.

"Listen to me, you insolent dog," he snarled. "Before I cut apart your miserable hide I'll give you a little lesson in ancient history and coming events. We people of the Rif have been neglected long enough. We have always been set apart, good to have around when there was fighting to be done and conquerors to be driven out, but otherwise ignored. But this is all at an end.

"Our mountains, long the fortress of the north and the gateway to Europe, will serve as avenues for new conquests from the east. Do you know your history, infidel? Do you know how the Moslem forces of the seventh and eighth centuries swept into Europe?"

I nodded. "They came across the Straits of Gibraltar," I said. "Where Morocco and Spain come closest together."

"Precisely," he said, eyes lighted with anticipation. "What you call Gibraltar we call after the Moslem emir who captured it, *Djebel Tarik* or Tarik's mountain. But Gibraltar is only a large rock. It is Spain we will strike."

"If you and your band are figuring on invading Spain, be my guests," I said, frowning.

I couldn't believe that was their scheme.

The Karminians would have recognized that for what it was, a hare-brained scheme not worth peddling to the Russians or to us. They wouldn't have even tried to peddle it.

No, it had to be something else and I felt a distinct chill at his next words.

"The ancient conquerors from Islam brought the world of the Far East with them in men, ideas and armies," he smiled. "I have effected such a mutually rewarding arrangement with our friends in the East."

The chill was getting chillier. "You mean the Chinese Reds?" I asked, trying to sound unconcerned.

He smiled again, like a satisfied cobra. "Exactly," he hissed. "Together, we are going to open up a new chapter in the history of the world."

I was remembering the sixth man at the old stable whose back I saw.

"Purely by accident one day, while I was in the foothills of the Rifs near Tetuan," he said. "I came across a fantastic engineering feat, one to rival the Pyramids and the Sphinx. I came across a tunnel, dug in the eighth century, from Morocco under the Straits of Gibraltar, to emerge in Spain. It was completed, except for the last few hundred feet upward to Spanish soil. Apparently it was never used, and no one living today knows why. But it is about to be used."

The words had an ominous ring to them, and I didn't really need to ask further, but I had to hear it through.

"You've tied up with the Chinese Communists," I said. "You're going to invade Spain through the tunnel."

My mind raced as I said it. The two countries were separated by only nine miles at one point.

A tunnel would afford the first surprise impact but the tunnel would only be a device. What its use would mean was the real explosive factor and the Karminians had recognized it at once.

Spain, the Mediterranean area, had remained a fairly stable region. It would be a real coup for the Chinese Communists to have trouble erupt there. A thousand ancient rivalries, alliances and emotional attitudes would assert themselves.

Led by the Rifs, with what would no doubt be termed Chinese volunteer fighters, it could even take on the aspect of the ancient Holy Wars of Moslem and Christian, stirring up a real kettle of undreamed-of problems.

The whole thing was fantastic in every aspect, fantastically wild and fantastically dangerous.

I could see now what El Ahmid had meant by history repeating itself.

He saw himself as a modern day Moslem conqueror with the Chinese as his helpers. But all the pieces were not in place. This kind of an operation took men, lots of men. How in hell were they getting here?

I looked at Marina, standing quietly, eyes riveted on the floor and then I gazed back at El Ahmid. I sighed casually, and grinned.

"A great story," I said. "You almost had me believing you. But you'd need men for such an operation, lots of men, and you'd first need to get them here, unseen and unobserved and that you can't do. Your whole story goes up in smoke right there."

El Ahmid smiled again, that self-satisfied, smug smile embroidered with contemptuous disdain.

"At this very moment," he said, "a huge camel caravan is nearing Oujda, the eastern end of the Taza Gap. The caravan, to anyone seeing it, belongs to a very wealthy slave trader, a dealer in women. There are over five hundred women, clothed in their *haiks* which, as you know, completely cover the wearer except for the eyes. He also has some two hundred guards in *djellabas* protecting the women."

"And the women inside their *haiks* are really Chinese soldiers, as are the guards," I finished.

"Exactly," he said. "Cargo ships at some twenty-five ports from Le Calle to Algiers discharged the men in small groups where arrangements were made to take them to an assembly spot in Sahara. There the caravan was made up and sent on its way. Five more such caravans are being made up and they will all arrive within the week. Of course, once the initial attack is made on Spanish soil, the need for such secretive moves will end. We have dedicated men ready to assassinate the King and major cabinet officers as soon as they hear of the fighting in Spain. All Morocco will be thrown into turmoil and I shall emerge as the leader."

I closed my ears to the rest of El Ahmid's rhetoric. He was convinced he was a reincarnation of the old Moslem conquerors who swept into Europe. That really was unimportant. He was being used by the Chinese. They didn't give a damn whether this wild scheme really succeeded in the final analysis.

Regardless of its eventual outcome it would create turmoil and havoc on a disastrous scale for the western powers and it would plunge them right into the middle of the Mediterranean basin. It would have a propaganda value of astronomic proportions on the many wavering and newly emerging nations.

The Russians, I knew, would be just as unhappy to see the Chinese Reds pop up smack in the middle of the North African-Southern European area. They had long ago decided that if there were to be Communist uprisings in any region they wanted it to be their brand, not that of the Chinese Reds.

I thought of what a shot-in-the-arm this stunt would give to the Red groups in Spain, Portugal and even France. The more I looked at this scheme, the more I realized that it could trigger repercussions all over the world.

El Ahmid had shut up, and I brought my attention back to him. He had gone over to Marina and reached out to touch one breast.

She shrank back and ran over to me.

"Such rare beauty," El Ahmid murmured as he gazed at Marina who tried to hide her naked breasts against me.

I pulled away from her.

"You're backing a loser," I said to her. "I can't help you now, baby. He can. He holds all the cards."

"An attack of rare common sense," El Ahmid said.

I callously ignored the shocked disbelief I saw in Marina's eyes and let my glance move casually to the Berber girl, standing to one side.

Her jaw was set grimly though she put on a seductive smile as she went over to El Ahmid and whispered something to him.

He spoke sharply to her in *tarrafit* without taking his eyes from Marina.

I saw anger flash in her eyes, and she snapped something back at him.

His answer was a sudden, whirling backhand blow that sent her sprawling on the floor. Before she could rise he was beside her and I saw his foot slam into her belly.

She gasped and lay on the floor.

"You do not tell El Ahmid what to do," he snarled at her.

The girl kept her head down as she fought to get her breath but I saw her eyes find Marina and there was hatred in them. She was reacting perfectly.

I could almost see the thoughts whirling around in her head. I'd give her one more push. I turned to Marina.

"Better be nice to him, baby," I said.

I put my hand on the small of her back and gave her a little push in Ahmid's direction.

"Get smart," I continued. "Play your cards right, and you'll come out all right."

Marina's eyes were deep pools of angry pain.

"You haven't a principle in your whole body, have you?" she shot back at me. "You'd do anything to try and save your neck. You'd bargain your mother away."

I shrugged and said nothing.

El Ahmid had watched the little scene, and he spoke out now, his voice taking on a hard edge. "Has your attack of common sense extended to telling me where Karminian hides."

I nodded. "I don't know the exact spot," I said. "But there's a place south of Casablanca, the black something-or-other."

"The Black Rocks," he cut in. *Les Roches Noires.*

"Yes, that's the name," I said. "He's hiding in that section, inside a small canning factory there."

It would take them at least a day to discover I'd made up the whole bit. By that time I'd be out of here, or it wouldn't make any difference anyhow.

"Now how about letting me go?" I asked. "I cooperated with you. You got what you wanted."

I glanced at Marina. "In fact, you got more than you started out to get."

"Your childish naïveté surprises me," El Ahmid said, that sneer of a smile on his face again. He snapped his fingers and two Rifs came forward to grab hold of me. "Take him away," the Rif leader said.

He felt his jaw gingerly. "I'll decide how to kill him in the morning. I want to think of something worthwhile for this one."

As they led me off I cast a quick glance back at the Berber girl.

She was standing to one side, watching El Ahmid start to sweet-talk Marina.

Marina would be all right for a while. He'd treat her with kid gloves for a few days, at least.

El Ahmid had picked a robe from the floor and was putting it around her shoulders.

I shot another glance at the Berber girl and I called out from the doorway.

"Tell him to let me go, Marina," I said.

The obvious implication of my appeal, that Marina would soon be in a position of influence, did just what I wanted. It was too much for the Berber girl, and I saw her turn and walk off, eyes narrowed in cold fury.

I grinned inwardly. After all these years I ought to know something about dames, I told myself, and female psychology was the same thing in all of them, whether they were from Manhattan or Marrakesh, Paris or Palermo, Athens or Addis Abbaba. I was counting on it to work once again.

# CHAPTER 6

I didn't land in the little cell again. This time it was a large, stone cellar with wall manacles. My wrists were locked into the manacles which kept me in an upright position, arms upraised.

It was a place built to hold many prisoners, but I was the only tenant at the moment. In a far corner I saw something that faintly resembled a wine press, but I knew the stains running down its sides were not grape juice.

In between watching scarabs, roaches and spiders scurry across the floor, I tried to formulate some kind of plan. Assuming things worked as I'd planned, I'd get out all right but after that what?

There was an American Consulate in Tangier. If I could reach it the AXE high-priority code would get me through to Hawk, and he could take it from there. But that would take time and it would also take me away from the scene.

If the first caravan was due to arrive, and five more on their way, it meant that trouble was ready to erupt, perhaps in a matter of days, even hours.

I had to get word to Hawk and I had to find that

tunnel. As I couldn't be in two places at one time I'd have to depend on Marina.

She wouldn't give me the time of day right now but that would change quickly enough, I knew. But would she carry through the rest of the way or, once on her own, would she take off and get away from the whole mess? After all, she wasn't even an American, and her stakes in all this were at best uncertain.

I smiled to myself. I'd give her a stake in it, a very personal stake that few women could resist investigating, at least. After all, she'd only just told me I hadn't a principle in my whole body. Maybe she was right.

I'd made my decisions and now I occupied my time in quietly straining at the wall manacles, working my wrists back and forth, trying to loosen them from their wall brackets. It was, of course, a pure waste of time, but it passed the day.

A couple of times I had a few visitors, Rif guards who stopped in to check on me. On the other side of the dungeon a small patch of reflected sunlight had lighted up the wall. When it disappeared I knew the day had ended, and little by little the darkness seeped down into the dungeon until I sat in near blackness. The only light was a fitful glow reflected from a wall torch around the corner of the corridor outside.

As the hours went on I was beginning to wonder if perhaps my confidence in the basic essentials of female psychology had been misplaced. I smiled wryly. It would be a hell of a time for it to go wrong.

And then my ears picked up the faint sound, soft footsteps in the darkness. I watched the arched entranceway into the room and saw the slender shape appear, halt and peer about.

"Over here," I whispered.

She came to me at once, kneeling down beside me. She still wore the bare midriff top and the diaphanous skirt.

"I was expecting you," I grinned in the dark.

Her French was heavy with a Berber accent.

"Then you promise to keep the bargain," she said. I nodded. "You promise to take her with you?" she asked.

"You set me free, and I'll take the girl with me, I promise," I said.

She reached up and turned the iron cross-bolts holding the manacles closed.

My arms dropped to my sides and I rubbed the circulation back into them.

"Where is the girl?" I asked.

"In the women's quarters," she answered, standing up. "I will take you to her."

We moved out into the corridor, and as we passed the wall torch I glanced at her face.

She was looking pleased, smug. No doubt she was contemplating her restoration to number one position again. In one simple stroke she would have gotten rid of an obvious threat and put herself back in as number one.

I got a bittersweet amusement out of being so right about her scheming, conniving little nature.

She led me up a narrow flight of steps, through a passageway barely large enough for one, over an open balcony looking down onto the courtyard and into one of the buildings forming the rear of the Casbah.

I heard the sounds of female voices and laughter

as we made our way through the semi-dark corridors.

We passed a lighted area, and I saw three girls, bare-breasted, wearing only floor-length, silk shifts, taking turns rubbing each other with some kind of oil. It would have been nice to stop and watch, but I followed the Berber girl as she hurried on soft *babouches* to another part of the house.

Motioning for me to hide in the shadows of a *mirhab*, an alcove-type recess facing in the direction of Mecca, she entered a room, and a moment later another girl came out and padded away down the corridor.

The Berber girl motioned to me again, appearing in the doorway, and I entered the room to see Marina slipping into her clothes.

Her eyes widened in astonishment when she saw me. I took her in my arms and grinned down at her.

"You didn't really think I was going to leave you here, did you, honey?" I asked.

She clung to me, relief flooding her eyes and she nodded. "Yes," she confessed. "Yes, I did. The way you acted and everything. That hurt more than being a prisoner here."

I patted her fanny. "I couldn't leave you here," I said. "I need you and you need me. We're a team, doll."

She nodded happily, and I turned to the Berber girl. Once again she was wearing that pleased-with-herself look, an actual smirk this time. She seemed almost too pleased, and suddenly I felt the hair at the back of my neck start to rise.

It was an unfailing, instinctive signal I had long ago learned never to disregard.

"Which way, now?" I asked her and she started out with a short motion of her hand.

I followed with Marina behind me.

El Ahmid's girl led us down a rear flight of stone steps into a kind of covered patio that led alongside the back of the building.

I noticed there were arched alcoves every ten feet or so along the wall.

She halted at the bottom of the steps and pointed to the dark structure at the other end of the long, covered patio.

"That is the stable," she whispered. "You will find two horses saddled and waiting inside."

"You go ahead," I said. "We'll follow."

"No," she answered, stepping back. "I can go no further."

"Why not?" I asked, grimly watching her.

"I . . . I might be seen here," she answered.

It was a phony answer and I thought of her smug expression again. Maybe she was more of a schemer than I'd suspected. Perhaps she was not only going to rid herself of a threat but add a little insurance for getting back as El Ahmid's favorite.

I grabbed her arm and twisted it behind her back with one hand while clapping my other hand over her mouth.

"Start walking," I hissed. "You first."

She tried to shake her head, but I was holding her so tight she couldn't even do that. Her eyes rolled sideways, showing the whites in helpless fright.

I shoved her out ahead of me at arm's length and started moving alongside the wall. We walked slowly and she tried to twist away. I tightened my grip and she stopped struggling. Her body was trembling beneath my vise-like hold as we passed the first alcove, then the second, then another and still another.

We were half-way to the stables, and I wondered if my intuition had sent out a false alarm this time when it happened, frighteningly fast even for my being on the alert.

We were but a pace from the next recessed alcove when the man leaped out, a long doubled-edge sword in his hand. He swung it with both hands as he leaped from the alcove, not stopping to look. Obviously, he was certain of what he'd find.

The tremendous swing almost cut the girl in half. I felt her body slam against mine and felt more than heard the sharp gasp of death that sucked from her mouth.

I let go and she collapsed instantly. I was diving over her, my hands reaching for the guard's throat before he could bring his blade back. I dug in silently, quickly and efficiently.

He clawed at my hands for a moment but I had him solidly. His eyes bulged, his hands fell away and I lowered him to the ground, dropping him half-over the girl.

I'd guessed correctly.

She had set it up with one of the guards, and it didn't take much imagination to see how she'd planned to have it work out.

He would have killed us both within moments. After that she would have started to scream the alarm. By the time anyone arrived at the scene we'd be two dead bodies, and both she and the guard would go up in El Ahmid's eyes.

If she'd just led us to safety, there'd possibly be questions raised as to how I'd escaped. This way she could embellish the whole thing with a story of how I'd slipped into the women's quarters and snatched Marina out before her very eyes. She'd followed us downstairs and screamed the alarm, and it would be so neat and pat.

Only it hadn't worked out that way, and I saw Marina staring transfixed at the two bodies. I scooped up the guard's heavy double-edge sword and grabbed Marina's hand, yanking her out of her shocked trance.

"This way," I hissed, pulling her along.

"What happened?" she asked as we ran.

"Long story," I smiled. "A case of attempted double-crossing, a technique that should never be tried by amateurs."

We reached the stable and slipped inside. It was full of horses, and, as I expected, there were no two Arabians saddled and waiting.

I saddled up two of the nearest stallions, carefully opened the stable door and started out.

"Bend low in the saddle," I said to Marina. "Make a small target of yourself and don't gallop until I do. Then give it everything you've got and follow me."

The big, arched entranceway was still open, one guard at each side of it. I walked the big, powerful stallion forward, letting him wheel around a few times on his own. Hunched low in the saddle, I knew the guards, at this distance, could see nothing more than a dark shape in the saddle. All they could make out were two horses and riders on them.

I edged the stallion toward the gate, keeping him at a frisky walk.

Marina was right behind me.

I played it cool and edged up still further. Coming out of the stables as we had, they were regarding us with no more than casual interest. Had we been approaching from outside they'd have had us in their rifle sights by now.

I turned the stallion's head toward the gate, looked back again to see that Marina was wheeling her horse in position, and dug my heels into his ribs. He flattened his ears back, leaped forward and took off like a desert windstorm.

I passed the two guards and was outside before they even got their rifles up. I was on my way down the steep path when I heard the sound of Marina's voice.

I looked back and saw her toppling from the saddle, one of the guards hanging onto her.

He had thought quickly and had seen there wouldn't be time for him to bring up his rifle and fire. He'd leaped forward, throwing himself at her as she rode past.

"Dammit!" I cursed, wheeling the stallion around.

I raced back and saw the one guard struggling with Marina. The other one, seeing me galloping back, tried to get his rifle up.

He never made it. I ran the stallion right at him and he had to leap aside. As he did so, I brought the double-edge sword down on his head. The thunking sound had the ring of utter finality to it.

The other one struggling with Marina threw her to the ground and brought his rifle around, but I was on him too fast.

I came down with the sword with all my strength.

He ducked it and I wheeled for another try but I saw he would have the rifle up to fire in a second.

I threw the sword, hard and down. It went into his chest like a lance.

Marina had mounted her horse before he hit the ground and we took off.

They'd be coming after us, but we had a head

start and they'd have to get lucky to pick which of the many passes we'd chosen to take.

But I wasn't about to take any chances. I kept up the breakneck pace until we were at the foot of the mountain range. We'd taken some perilously steep trails to cut down as straight as we could and now I halted at the edge of the Taza Gap.

To the east, the camel caravan would be approaching from Algeria or Southern Morocco. To the west of the gap, Tangiers and the American Consulate.

I dismounted and pulled Marina down beside me.

"You heard what El Ahmid is planning," I told her. "He's got to be stopped. I'm going to give you a secret code signal. You ride to Tangiers, don't stop for anything, ride right to the American Consulate there. Give the code signal to him and ask him to call AXE headquarters for you. He'll do it because of the code signal. When you get AXE headquarters, tell the person on the phone the whole story. Got that so far?"

She nodded and I went on.

"Most important," I said, "is to tell them about the camel caravan that will enter the Taza Gap. Tell them I said to run with the ball."

She frowned.

"That means to do whatever is necessary to meet the situation," I said.

"Where will you be, Nick?" she asked.

"I'm going to find me a spot somewhere and wait for that caravan," I answered. "If my people don't make it, I might still find a way to do something. I don't know what but I'm sure as hell going to try."

I looked down at her and remembered my thoughts about giving her a personal stake in all this. Now it was my time to buy a little insurance. I pressed my lips down on hers and held her breasts, pressing both hands against them. I ran my thumbs gently across their tips, feeling her nipples swell beneath the fabric of the dress.

"Remember what I said about needing each other?" I asked. "After you get to my people, when this is over, maybe we can make this a permanent team?"

I saw her eyes deepen and she nodded, holding me tight.

"Now get going, honey," I whispered in her ear, a little reluctant to let go of those soft, enticing breasts myself. "Every second counts."

I helped her mount, kissed her again and watched her go off. When she was out of sight and the first gray tint of dawn began to spread across the sky, I turned the stallion around and headed east along the edge of the Taza Gap.

The sky continued to lighten, and as it did I saw the flat stretch of land along which I rode, the historic road for conquerors from the East. The Taza Gap lay between the Rif range and the mountains known as the Middle Atlas. Through its wide swath, ancient legions had traveled from east to west and west to east and left their mark on the land itself.

I passed the ruins of ancient villages where Roman garrisons had been quartered, the unmistakable relics of Roman architecture an echo of their days of glory.

The road led up high into the mountains but still remained a natural highway between the two mountain ranges.

I stayed close along the northern edge, watching carefully as the sun rose high in the sky.

El Ahmid and his men would be out, coming this way, I knew. They might travel a distance in the Rif mountains and then cut down onto the Taza Gap as I had done with Marina, but sooner or later they would have to appear. Knowing I'd escaped, he had only one thing to do, meet the caravan and advance his timetable before I could summon help.

I had to halt to water the horse a few times but other than that I rode steadily, grateful for the deep-chested stamina of the Arabian under me.

It was late afternoon when I neared the eastern end of the gap. I wheeled the horse up into the Rif foothills, found a sheltered spot behind a circle of large boulders and put the stallion out of sight.

Climbing up onto the boulders, I flattened out and began to watch from my makeshift falcon's nest. I could see a good distance down the gap in either direction, and I wondered how Marina had made out. I was pretty sure she had kept on with her mission, but I wasn't at all sure they hadn't cut her off before she got very far.

Only time would tell, and, as I waited in the heat of the blistering sun, I realized that I was pretty damn helpless. I hadn't a revolver, a rifle, a dagger or a toothpick.

If Marina hadn't made it, how the hell did I expect to stop an armed camel caravan of some seven hundred men plus those El Ahmid would bring with him to meet them? I'd have to meet a genie in a bottle, I said to myself. That or find Aladdin and his magic lamp.

My idle thoughts were cut off by a cloud of dust from the west. The cloud grew and materialized into El Ahmid and his men. There were some two hundred of them, I estimated, riding like hell with the

Rif leader in the forefront. They were just about opposite me when I saw El Ahmid raise his hand and
rein up to a halt.

I peered in the other direction to see the camel
caravan approaching, the stately, unhurried motion
of the camels somehow reminiscent of a royal
procession. The caravan stretched out farther back
than I could see, and I saw the double rows of camels in the center carrying the *haik*-clad "women,"
two on a camel.

The armed guards, equally hidden in their *bur-
nooses* and voluminous *djellabas*, lined either side of
their precious cargo.

El Ahmid and two of his men raced forward to
meet the caravan while the rest of his force stayed
behind.

I saw them hold a hurried conference and then a
series of shouted commands was passed back along
the caravan.

I saw the camels suddenly come to life and begin
to move forward with surprising speed. When they
neared me I saw they were using the *mehari*, the
sand-colored fast dromedaries used by the troopers
of the Camel Corps.

I waited, watching, as the caravan moved past
and went on down the Taza Gap, headed westward.

I mounted up and began a careful pursuit, staying
in the narrow passes of the foothills.

The camels, even the fleetest of them, were slow
compared to the horses, and the entire caravan
moved at a relatively slow pace. Even negotiating
the ups and downs of the mountain roads I had no
trouble staying with them.

But now nightfall was approaching, and I was beginning to worry. I'd seen no sign of help arriving. If

darkness fell, they'd keep going and no doubt make it to the trail up Mount Dersa and El Ahmid's Casbah. From there, it was probably not far to the entrance to the tunnel.

I still had the two tubes of paint in my pocket. If you ignited them in the tube, in concentrated form, they were as powerful as two sticks of dynamite each, but even that, out here in the wide-open spaces of the Taza Gap, would mean little.

Suddenly, as I rode over the crest of a narrow path, I saw the caravan and the small army of Rifs come to a halt. Up ahead, a cloud of dust rose once again and it grew quickly into what was at first a brilliant red patch. It soon separated itself into the uniforms of the crack horsemen of the Royal Guards, each on a gray Arabian stallion and each carrying a long lance along with the regular rifles and handguns.

I counted four battalions, a good number of men but not even half of those making up the Rif brigade and the camel caravan.

I said a silent thanks to Marina. She obviously had made it, but I wondered if she had forgotten to mention how many would be in the caravan.

I watched the Royal Guards draw closer and saw that they had spread their ranks across the entire Taza Gap, from side to side. They rode forward at a slow trot, each one a thin line of red.

I had halted at the top of a short path that would lead me down into the middle of the caravan. Either the approaching horsemen were supermen or they were damned confident.

They maintained their slow trot, and now I saw El Ahmid whipping his men into a frenzy, riding back and forth among them.

I saw rifles brandished aloft, along with the curved Moorish daggers and heavy double-edged swords. Then I heard a sharp, staccato sound, the chopping sound of rotary blades in the air.

I looked up, shielding my eyes against the sun, to see four, five, six huge helicopters coming down behind the caravan. I saw more of them approaching and I saw the markings on them. They were U.S. Navy cargo 'copters from one of the Mediterranean-based carriers. The first one had already landed and opened its bay, and I saw more red uniforms on more gray stallions racing out and down the ramp.

The 'copters were landing another four battalions at least behind the caravan, boxing El Ahmid and his "slave girls" in between them. The 'copters took to the air instantly, and the Royal Guards went into their slow trot at once, also forming the same straight lines across the width of the gap.

I heard a whistle, and the slow trot changed into a fast trot.

El Ahmid had frantically dispatched half his men to the rear of the caravan to meet the attack from that quarter.

At another whistle the Royal Guards broke into a full gallop. I watched them lower their lances to the "charge" position. They ploughed into El Ahmid's men like the prongs of some huge pitchfork digging into a bale of hay, shifting their lines at the very last moment to tighten up their formation and hit with double the impact.

The battle was joined with a tremendous roar and the sound of rifle fire mingled with the coarse shouts of men and the galloping of hoofs. The Chinese posing as women were not equipped with arms, and they were bolting in terror, leaping from the camels and attempting to flee as the Royal Guards cut through El Ahmid's men and attacked the caravan.

It was time to join the fun. I spurred my horse down the narrow path and landed smack in the middle of things, coming along just as a Royal Guardsmen impaled one of the rifle-carrying guards on a lance.

The man toppled from the camel and I reached down to scoop up his rifle. It was a Chinese version of the M-16.

I got off a good burst that caught two of the fleeing Chinese and one of El Ahmid's men. I fought my way through the wheeling, milling confusion of camels, horses and men fleeing on foot. I managed to grab one of the curved Moorish daggers from the belt of a dead Rif as he dangled from his saddle and stuck it into my belt.

As usually happens, the efficient, trained tactics of the professionals were making themselves felt. The Royal Guardsmen roared in and out of the shouting, wild-eyed fighters of El Ahmid's men with unspectacular but deadly effect.

The Rifs, natural warriors and fierce fighters, were unsurpassed at their kind of hit-and-run tactics, the roaring attack of unexpected fury. Against the trained cavalry tactics of the red-uniform Guardsmen they were more sound than fury, more energy than efficiency.

The "slave girls" were being mowed down as they tried to flee. Those managing to get away would be either rounded up later or fall prey to the harshness of the mountains on either side of them.

But El Ahmid was in there someplace, and as I wheeled off to the side to get a better view of the battle I saw him, battling well against two Guardsmen, avoiding their thrusts and cutting them down with a brilliant maneuver.

I spurred my horse forward to cut across after him when I saw him turn, wave an arm at three of his lieutenants, and start to race from the scene of the battle. The Guardsmen had more than they could handle. They had no one to spare to chase after the fleeing Rifs.

I edged my way along the side of the battle, pausing to exchange rifle fire with one of the Chinese still astride his camel.

He came down at me in an awkward gait, rifle raised to his shoulder and firing. On a horse he'd have easily sent at least two shots into me but on the camel it was like firing from the deck of a pitching, tossing ship. The shots went around my ears, and I brought him down with one fast return.

El Ahmid and his three Rifs were still in sight but disappearing fast down the road.

I took after them, content to keep them in sight. I didn't want to catch up yet.

They cut into the mountains on the other side of Taza, leaving the Taza Gap and going up along the Rif itself.

I followed suit. If they knew I was following them they gave no sign of it. I kept my distance, staying just close enough to keep them in sight from time to time as they raced up and around and through the narrow Rif passages.

It was almost dark now, and I knew we were getting back near Mount Dersa when I saw them suddenly turn off the trail and enter a single-file gorge.

I went down after them and into the narrow, high-sided path. It was long and continuously narrow, and I realized it was a deep cut through the mountain, running toward the coastline.

I couldn't see them any longer, and I increased my speed, pausing every so often to listen for the sound of their horses up ahead.

The narrow gorge widened out finally by a clump of orange trees in what appeared to be a small mountain valley. I galloped along the road and turned a sharp corner.

A body dropped on me like the proverbial ton of bricks, and I went flying from the saddle. On the ground, the man lost his grip for a moment and I twisted away to see it was one of the Rifs.

He'd dropped back, climbed onto a ledge at the corner and waited. He pulled out his dagger and came for me.

I ducked the first slice and avoided the second one. I'd almost forgotten I carried one stuck in my belt, and I brought it out with a sweeping motion. The curved dagger was not a weapon I was used to and against an experienced fighter it could be worse than no weapon at all.

I tried a swipe with it and he deftly fended it and came around with a slashing blow that almost ended the fight. I felt the tip of the blade nick my throat as it went by. I went into a crouch and circled.

He brought his blade upward in an arc and then back and forth in two quick motions and once again I twisted away with not more than a fraction of an inch to spare.

Angry, I tossed the damn dagger to one side and faced him. I saw his broken teeth flash as he smiled in anticipation.

He rushed me, which was what I was waiting for.

I dropped low and came up inside his curved swing with a hard right to the belly.

As he grunted I grabbed his arm, applied pressure and gave him a hip-flip. He went crashing down onto the ground. Before he could gather himself, I scooped up the dagger from where I'd tossed it and brought it down in a crashing, curving blow. I watched his head separate from his body.

"That one's for Aggie Foster," I muttered.

My stallion had halted nearby. I retrieved my rifle and started off at a gallop.

El Ahmid and the other two would be somewhere ahead, waiting, I knew.

I rode on for a while and then took to my feet, moving silently, cautiously along the pathway. The mountain rose to the right of me in a series of rocky formations and the path curved and twisted. Suddenly I heard the neigh of a horse ahead.

I moved forward slowly, keeping to the deep shadows alongside the steep rock sides of the mountain. I saw them waiting, El Ahmid and the other two. Taking my rifle, I checked the chamber and uttered a mixed oath and expression of thanks. There was but one bullet in it. I had intended to step out and start blazing away. It would have been a very unhappy surprise for me.

"I won't wait any longer," I heard El Ahmid say. "Muhad would be here by now if something hadn't gone wrong. Perhaps they are both dead."

The other two nodded solemnly, and I watched as El Ahmid walked over to the side of the mountain and began to press his hands along the stones.

Suddenly, with a groaning, rumbling noise, one of the stones began to move slowly, opening up in door-like fashion. Shades of Ali Baba and the Forty

Thieves, I muttered to myself. I stayed quiet as El Ahmid and the other two got on their horses and disappeared into the mountain. In a moment the stone began to move again and with a rumbling groan went back into place.

I moved out into the open. They were inside the tunnel. Whether they were going to hide out there or ride through it and into Spain, they'd be there a while. I waited, giving them plenty of time to move deep into the tunnel. I didn't want them to hear the door open again.

Finally, I went over to the stone wall of the mountain and began to press against it as I'd seen El Ahmid do. Nothing happened and I almost felt like saying "Open, Sesame." I started over again, this time pressing harder, moving along the rock inch by inch. Half-way across a smooth section I felt a slight movement.

I stepped back quickly and watched the rock slide open again. I mounted my horse and rode in, expecting utter darkness. I found the tunnel dimly lighted but still lighted by a series of small light bulbs hung from the ceiling and obviously operated by a battery generator.

I walked the stallion down the slope of the tunnel, surprisingly wide, and my eyes took in the old wood beams overhead, most of them shored up by fresh timbers. The tunnel sloped downward steeply for a long while and then leveled off.

I spurred the Arabian on to a fast trot, risking the echo that resounded in the tunnel. A dank clamminess was in the air now, and I guessed I was underwater.

They had to be ahead someplace. There was nowhere else to go.

I pressed on, pausing to listen. I heard nothing and decided to go forward faster. As I galloped through the tunnel I saw them ahead, waiting, facing me. I halted some ten yards from them.

"So, American," El Ahmid said. "I underestimated your cleverness. But you have just entered your tomb."

"Maybe," I answered. "May it'll serve for all of us."

I glanced up at the stone and dirt roof, the walls of stone and hard-baked clay. They had survived centuries, held together by the chemical knowledge of an ancient culture, but I had my doubts if they would survive a good-sized explosion. All it would take would be enough of a shock tremor. The pressure of the water outside would do the rest, and once it caved in the whole thing would go.

I looked at the trio in front of me. If they made it to Spain, they'd still be the only ones who knew of the existence of the tunnel. I knew El Ahmid would merely bide his time for another attempt, perhaps this time with different backers. I couldn't let them get away, no matter what it cost.

This ancient feat of Arab engineering was a kind of time-bomb from the pages of history, a legacy left by the old Moslem conquerors. It would be ironic if, after hundreds of years, they would have the last laugh on the western world.

El Ahmid would see to it if he were left to escape. He was inflamed with his own sense of destiny, a man too dangerous to let get away.

I had the dagger and a rifle with one bullet in it. Not much to fight with. The tubes of paint in my pocket were the best bet. They'd cause a helluva explosion, enough, I felt certain, to bring the old tunnel to a crashing, water-filled end. Would there be a chance to get out before it collapsed around my ears? The chances were more no than yes.

"Take him," El Ahmid said quietly and I saw them start to move toward me, each one of them drawing his long, curved dagger.

I backed the horse down the tunnel and did some fast calculating. I had two tubes of the explosive paint. If one could wreck the tunnel and bring it crashing down, with the sea pouring in, there'd never be time enough to outride the rushing water and escape via the entrançe. They'd try it, I knew, but they'd never make it.

But I'd still have one tube left and a half a minute, perhaps a whole minute, before the tunnel filled with water. I thought back to what I knew of the laws of water pressure and counter-force. I knew what Hawk had told me about the paint, that once lighted it would go off underwater as well as on land.

What the hell, I muttered, it was worth the risk. I could afford to be philosophical. There wasn't anything else left to be. But if I had a million-to-one chance I had first to avoid getting sliced up three ways.

El Ahmid and the other two were advancing on me.

I wheeled the stallion around, galloped back a few yards and then turned and charged them. They halted and waited for me, their vicious daggers upraised, ready to carve me up as I tried to run the gauntlet through them.

I saw El Ahmid's smile of disdain once again. I kept the stallion at full gallop, heading right for them and I drew my own dagger to make it look good. The horse's head was level with their steeds' when I slipped from the saddle and swung around under the horse's neck in an old trick taught me by a movie stunt rider years ago.

I heard the three daggers clank against each other as they swiped at empty air. Once through them I swung back into the saddle and leaped off the horse while he was still running. He went on down the tunnel as I grabbed one of the paint tubes from my pocket. I held my lighter against it and it flared up, a lovely rose madder. I had some fifteen seconds leeway before it ignited.

I tossed it at the three Rifs who backed off in wariness.

They fell backward as it went off with a deafening roar.

I wasn't really watching them, anyway. My eyes were on the wall as the concentrated explosion erupted. I was sent flying but I was braced for it and let my body roll relaxed. I came up on one knee, my eyes focusing on the wall.

I saw the shower of dirt and clay cascade into the tunnel, followed by the torrent of water. Huge cracks appeared on both sides now and spread instantly in all directions. Dirt, followed by water, erupted from every new crack. And then, with a deafening roar, the whole damned thing opened up, and a rushing, leaping torrent of water raced into the tunnel to spread out in both directions.

I was caught up in it and swirled upward toward the top of the tunnel. I swam against the onrushing current, back toward the main opening. There was still some four feet of air space between the rising water and the roof.

I caught a glimpse of tossed bodies on the other side of the cascading water, and I knew El Ahmid's dream had gone to join those of other conquerors in history. There wasn't much more than a foot of air space left now.

I took out the second tube, lit it and dropped it into the water beneath me. I knew it was heavy enough to sink slowly, at least. I waited the fifteen seconds, took a deep breath and forced air into my eardrums and sinuses.

The explosion did what I'd calculated it would do. I felt myself lifted as by a tremendous wet hand and sent hurtling upward through the water, out through the opening of the tunnel roof. The pressure was terrible. I felt my body grow tight, my lungs burning, straining as the explosion forced me upward through the water like a torpedo.

I felt my shoes rip away, and then my clothes tear. The pressure was getting more than the human body could bear and I could feel the veins and blood vessels expanding to the bursting point when I shot into the air. My lungs hurt terribly as I gulped the first breath of air. It went down into them like ice water, and I felt dizzy. I managed to tread water and strike out feebly.

Finally, I floated over on my back and let the current carry me from the seething, churning water. I floated until I felt enough strength returning to my arms and legs, until I began to feel as though I might stay together.

Slowly, swimming with easy, deliberate strokes, I headed back for the Moroccan coastline. Luckily, I hadn't come that far through the tunnel, and when I finally reached the sand, I collapsed and lay there, a dark, still shape in the night.

I lay there a long time and then slowly got to my feet. I couldn't help but think of my first landing on the shores of Morocco and I looked carefully around to see that I was alone.

The walk up the beach was a gentle slope, for which I was thankful. I found a road and started to walk west toward Tangiers. When morning came I was still on the road. I waved down a jeep I saw approaching. It turned out to be filled with Moroccan soldiers, searching for Chinese fugitives along the coastline.

At my story they spun the jeep about, and we raced for Tangiers and the American Consulate.

# CHAPTER 7

I identified myself and got a hot shower and a suit of clothes as I waited for the call to Hawk to be put through. Things had happened as I'd surmised, I found out.

Marina had to talk fast to make her story believed, but the code signal I'd given her did the trick. On the phone, Hawk filled me in on the details.

"From the girl's story," his voice crackled over the phone, "I knew you were up the creek without a paddle. The Moroccan government had the proper forces to cope with the situation but not the transportation. We had the means of transportation but not the forces, so we put our heads together and you saw the results. I don't mind telling you I had to talk fast to convince then I wasn't on LSD and dreaming the whole thing up."

"I wish you had," I answered. "It was a puzzler with a very nasty kicker."

"By the way, we retrieved Hugo and Wilhelmina from the Russians you scattered around Casablanca," he said. "Take a day off, N3. Relax and enjoy the sun there."

"Your generosity overwhelms me once again," I said. "So much so that I'm going to take the whole damn week off."

"Who is she?" Hawk asked. "The girl who contacted us?"

"Yes," I said. "I've got to cancel an insurance policy."

"Are you all right, N3?" Hawk said, sudden concern in his voice. "Did you say something about an insurance policy?"

"I'll explain when I see you," I grinned and hung up.

As I walked out of the Consulate I saw a tall, long-limbed figure move toward me, her hair now beautifully combed and in place, once again the same delicate yet sensual creature I'd first met that night at Karminian's apartment. Her arm crept into mine and her lips brushed my cheek.

"Oh, Nick," she said. "You don't know what hell it was waiting and wondering if you'd come back alive."

"I've got to thank you for that, or at least for part of it," I said.

"I kept remembering what you'd said when I left," she murmured. "About us being a team, a permanent team."

I grimaced inwardly and looked at those deep, dark eyes.

Her dress, soft beige with a deep slit at the neck, outlined the round provocative beauty of her breasts.

"About what I said then, Marina," I began. "I want to talk to you about that."

"Not here, Nick," she said, pressing her finger to

my lips. "Let us go back to Casablanca, to my place. I would like it better there."

I shrugged. Maybe it would be better that way. Maybe I could make up for what I was going to have to tell her. Nobody likes being a bastard, even when they know they've been one in a good cause.

We rode back to Casablanca in an army car the Moroccan government put at my disposal as a gesture of gratitude. When we reached her place she opened the door and spun into my arms, her eyes bright and glistening.

I wanted to make love to her, but that would only be compounding things, adding insult to injury. God, if only she weren't so damned desirable.

We'd made small talk all the way back from Tangiers, as if both of us were avoiding the issue.

I knew I sure as hell was, but I also knew that I couldn't put it off indefinitely.

"Marina," I began. "About what I said in the mountains."

I never got more than that out when the sharp sound of a door being kicked open made me spin around. I whirled to see Karminian coming out of the bedroom, disheveled, gaunt and red-eyed with a big .357 Magnum in his hand.

"I knew you'd come back sometime," he said to Marina. "I didn't expect you'd come back with him."

"Anton," she said, starting for him. "Oh, it's good to see you. You're alive, thank God."

He laughed harshly. "Traitor . . . bitch," he shot out at her. "Liar. Daughter of the devil. I live but no thanks to you."

"Now, hold on, pal," I said slowly, watching the gun in his hand stay trained on Marina's abdomen.

"She was trying to help you. In fact, I talked her into it."

He swung the gun on me. "Then it is fitting you both die together," he said. "I came here and waited to kill her. Now you can die with her."

"Anton," Marina said. "Please listen to me. I was only doing what was best for you. I wasn't betraying you."

He snarled at her again, an oath in Armenian, this time.

I sized it up quickly.

He'd flipped his wig. It probably hadn't taken too much to do it. Based on what Marina had told me of their relationship, he had a weird approach to women anyway. It didn't take much to convince him that she was a traitor, a creature of evil.

He was a strange one, as I'd told her once before, an introverted ascetic, and if I knew the type he was an egomaniac. They were always certain of their superiority because of their spiritual approach to life.

If I was going to stop that cannon in his hand from going off I'd have to reach him in that way.

"There's no sense in trying to fool him, Marina," I said. "He knows we lie. I think you'd better ask his forgiveness."

Marina shot me a frowning glance but this time she caught my meaning and turned to Karminian.

"I'd get on my knees, Marina," I said. "You need to beg for his forgiveness."

Marina moved toward him and dropped to her knees, her head bowed contritely. "Can you forgive me, Anton?" she asked.

I watched him, waiting, as he looked down at her with the god-like severity of the just judging the unjust.

"I can forgive you, Marina," he said. "But will the Lord?"

She raised her eyes and looked up at him. "Let me feel the touch of your hand on my head, Anton," she said. She was doing a great job.

He half-smiled in merciful kindness. He shifted the Magnum to his left hand and reached out to touch her head. It was all the moment I needed.

I dived and grabbed his gun. The cannon went off in my ear, but I had him against the wall, pounding his head on the baseboard. I heard the clatter as the gun fell to the floor from his hand. I crossed a hard right, and he lay still.

Picking up the gun, I dialed the police, and we waited till they collected him. I told them to call the Army and turn him over to them. When they'd cleared out, Marina came over to me again, her arms encircling my neck.

After the way she'd handled Karminian, I felt even more indebted to her and more of a bastard. There would be no easy way but to plunge in.

"I've got to straighten something out with you," I said. "About what I said about our being a permanent team."

"I've not thought of anything else since you said it, Nick," she smiled.

Dammit to hell, I groaned. Why do they always have to make it more difficult

"Look, honey," I tried again. "It would be great, but it can't work out. Not now, not for me. I said it to you then because I . . . well, I felt I had to. I didn't mean it. I'm being honest about it, Marina. I didn't mean it."

She looked at me and pursed her lips. Suddenly she was laughing, a deep, throaty, rich laugh.

"What's so funny?" I asked.

"You," she said. "I know you didn't mean it. I knew it then. It's not in character with you, Nick. Maybe you might have fooled some girls but not me."

I recalled how damned perceptive she'd been when I first met her. I felt myself getting a little annoyed at the way she laughed at me.

"You weren't so damned smart when I told you to play cards right with El Ahmid," I said. "You believed me then. You accused me of doing anything to save my own neck."

"That's right," she said. "I believed you because that *was* in character. You would do anything to save your own neck if saving your neck meant completing your mission. You would bargain me, or anyone else away, if it had to be done for the sake of your objective. Of course I believed you then."

I looked at her.

She was laughing at me again, her deep eyes dancing pools.

"Then why'd you come back here with me?" I asked.

"Because I wanted you to stay in character," she said, her eyes twinkling.

She came over to me and slid her hand inside my shirt. Her fingers were soft messengers of desire and her mouth, open and eager, found mine. She had my shirt open and her hand worked at my belt buckle.

I lifted her up and carried her into the bedroom.

"I'll stay in character," I promised her, with a tinge of savagery creeping into my voice.

Marina had her dress off and her body pressed against mine. She was filled with desire, once again, but now the burst-dam pent-up desperation was gone. It had been replaced by a sensuous rapture all its own, a gliding, smooth, magnificent body that set its own rhythms and made its own time.

Marina held my head down to her breasts and cried out in ecstasy as my lips found their soft tips. She thrust upward until it seemed she wanted all of her firm, creamy breasts to be held in my mouth.

I caressed her with my hands, with my lips, with my tongue, and she was a woman transported to another world.

We made love slowly, gently, and then with feverish desire but never harshly, never crudely.

Marina hadn't a crude bone in her body, but then, all of a sudden, she changed.

I'd been stroking her very being in increasing rhythm and she had lain moaning and gasping, and then suddenly she flung her body upward, seized my hand and held it to her and her lips turned back in a wild smile and I saw the wild gypsy creature I'd ridden beside through the Rif mountains.

"Come to me, Nick," she half-screamed. "Come to me."

I rolled my body on hers, and she seized my shoulder in her teeth. It was a pain of pleasure and her cries were protests of ecstasy.

The day turned into night, and our bodies finally lay side by side, spent, empty of physical strength but filled with the powers of the senses.

Marina's breasts rested on my chest and she looked up at me.

"When it's like this," she said, "who cares if it's permanent?"

It was a good question. I made a note to remember it for future use.

THE END

# Nick Carter: the world's biggest selling spy series